Ashley Grey's UNEXPECTED LOVE

by
PALMA EHL ALLISON

To Aunt Thelma: I hope you enjoy my story. Thinking of you often

Love,
Palma Allison

PublishAmerica
Baltimore

© 2010 by Palma Ehl Allison.
All rights reserved. No part of this book may be reproduced, stored in a retrieval system or transmitted in any form or by any means without the prior written permission of the publishers, except by a reviewer who may quote brief passages in a review to be printed in a newspaper, magazine or journal.

First printing

All characters in this book are fictitious, and any resemblance to real persons, living or dead, is coincidental.

PublishAmerica has allowed this work to remain exactly as the author intended, verbatim, without editorial input.

Hardcover 978-1-4489-3347-1
Softcover 978-1-4489-4190-2
PUBLISHED BY PUBLISHAMERICA, LLLP
www.publishamerica.com
Baltimore

Printed in the United States of America

In Loving Memory of my Father

DOUGLAS EHL

April 1934 – November 2009

Acknowledgments

Many thanks must go to my very supportive and patient husband Bruce Allison along with our children Samantha, Austyn and Dustin. Also very supportive are my mother Leona Ehl and my husband's parents Bill and Lorraine Allison.

I spent many hours on the telephone reading parts and asking for opinions from my daughter and mother and it is them that encouraged or first suggested I consider having my story published. Special thanks to Laura Chivers in her proof reading and help with minor changes needed.

I would also like to thank the Librarian in Greenwood. She has been very helpful in bringing in books from other libraries. Never underestimate the power of the library.

I cannot forget to thank all those from PublishAmerica for accepting my manuscript and the work they put into making my book a reality.

1
April 1869

It has been a long journey and stepping down off the coach to finally stand on solid ground almost feels strange. Looking at the unfamiliar faces and surroundings around the station I now begin to realize the situation I have put myself in and what I must now summon up the strength to do. The thought of it makes me feel overwhelmed and the sky begins to spin. When I wake up I am disoriented and lost. I can hear the crackling of a fire in a fire place and I feel the warmth. Some things begin to come to me as memories from a dream that didn't seem real. Looking into the face of young lady wearing a crisp white servant's apron and bonnet I am confused. I try to speak but the words are lost on a week and tired voice that doesn't seem to be my own. My head hurts so much and everything is so confusing.

Miss my name is Maggie and I am to summon the Lady of this house upon your awakening." With that she leaves the room and I blink a couple of times just to try to figure out what has happened, and where I am. My head feels like it is in a thick fog and everything is so hazy. I remember now, being helped into a different carriage than the one I had arrived in, and vaguely remember stairs and a hallway. What I do realize is this is no Hotel or hospital but rather it is a very beautifully decorated room. The hard wood furnishings are done in rich, dark tones elaborately carved giving the room a warm comfortable feeling. The finishing touches from the paintings and tapestries down to the rugs and long beautiful curtains pulled open to reveal a spring day slowly coming to an end reveal a woman's personal touch. This room would have been pleasant to be in as an invited guest and under better circumstances. But in my circumstances I feel like an intruder surrounded by strangers. I close my eyes again as I hear voices in the hall, and then the door is opened.

An older woman enters. Wearing a dark burgundy gown bustled at the back she is tall and stands straight. Ashley remembers her from the coach. She is probably in her late forties maybe early fifties. Her hair mostly blond is pulled up away from her face to reveal blue eyes and features that are soft and kind. More of how I came to be here comes to me but it seems to be in bits and pieces like a puzzle taking shape.

A gentleman enters along with her and I am beginning to come to my senses more. The older woman comes to the side of the bed and re-introduces herself as Lady Elizabeth Thatcher, the woman I had spent so much time on the train and then on the coach with now explains that I had blacked out at the station. She had arranged for me and my belongings to be brought to her home and now to be examined by the doctor. At this the young gentleman comes forward and introduces himself as Dr. Denley. Ashley guesses him to be about six feet tall and probably in his late twenties. He has short dark hair, clean shaven, brown eyes and dimples. He was definitely pleasing to the eyes. Opening His black bag he takes out his stethoscope and adjusts it in his ears, and he listens to my heart, he asks me to lean forward and he listens to my lungs as well. The stethoscope is cold to the touch and I shiver a little. Then he checks my eyes and reflexes. Asking the others to leave the room he now has me lift the soft white night gown I am wearing.

(I faintly remember being helped into it...something about falling into a puddle of water and wanting to get me into something dry so I wouldn't catch the death of a cold. I must have hit my head when I fell and that explains the headache I have.) He wanted to listen for the baby and feel how it is positioned.

"I am due to have the baby in about three or four week's time." I feel it necessary to break the silence.

"Your baby sounds fine but I don't want anymore fainting episodes; falling to the ground is not the safest thing for you or your baby. In your condition and blacking out so easily I strongly advise you have complete bed rest. You should have your husband contacted so he can arrange his affairs to have you properly cared for at home, Mrs.____?"

Tears now well up in my eyes and looking down at my hands resting on my big tummy to avoid his watchful eyes I mutter, "My name is Ashley Grey." Again I realize the terrible situation I am in; how I made the decision to leave with no time to make any arrangements. I hadn't had time to even think things through properly. The tears do not go unnoticed by the doctor. Now looking again very seriously he asks me what the problem is and bursting into sobs I begin to spill in a shaky and sometimes almost inaudible sound the loss of my husband and that I have arrived in this town a stranger.

With the night gown gently pulled down into place and the covers pulled back up and tucked in, he excuses himself from the room and again the voices in the hall can be heard but not the content of the conversation. Elizabeth enters the room with the Doctor and again comes to the side of the bed. I begin sitting up and falter for words, "I have to go; I'm sorry to have put you to so much trouble. I need to get back to town and get a hotel room before night fall." I finish my sentence in desperation and want nothing more than to become invisible. You will do no such thing," she informs me. "You are in no shape to be getting up out of this bed, let alone wandering about town trying to find a hotel room. It has already been decided that you will stay in this house as a guest and it will not do to protest."

I give her a weak smile and a thank-you. I am actually relieved that I don't need to leave now with the way I am feeling. I can think it out more clearly tomorrow after I have rested.

Summoning Maggie back into the room she is told to see to anything that I need for my comfort and to see to it that I am resting as to the doctor's orders. "A cup of tea and a bit of soup or a sandwich should be brought from the kitchen for her as I know the last meal she had has been too many hours ago to think about especially in her condition." With a last caution by the doctor the room becomes quiet and I close my eyes again and try to comprehend the situation I am in, and the kindness of an older woman who for the most part had said very little to me on the coach.

Lady Elizabeth walked with the doctor to the door and in a kindly voice he asks her if she feels up to what might be in store. "It doesn't look like that young lady is going to carry that baby for too much longer and the rest is crucial. She doesn't seem to have anyone here and I don't know what would cause a person to make such a trip in her condition. Apart from what she told me about being widowed recently she has not said what brings her here."

With a slight nod of the head Lady Elizabeth agreed that this would be better than any hotel. "Maybe she'll be good company and I have nothing but time to spend in this lonely house."

"If it gets to be too much for you be sure to tell me so we can figure something out for Ms. Grey. I'll be by tomorrow to check on her." On those words he climbed into his carriage and disappeared from sight as he directed his horse down the drive.

Making her way up to her bedroom Lady Elizabeth realized how tired she was. It had been a long day for her as well. Catching Maggie on the stairs she asked that a tray be brought up for her with something to eat and a cup of tea. "I'm going to turn in early this evening. I'm quite tired. Tell me, how is our young guest Ms. Grey doing?"

"She is resting quietly for now Mam. I'll have a tray up for you in a few minutes, and I'll keep a watch on our guest in case she is in need of anything."

Once in her room Elizabeth sat at her vanity and let her hair down. Brushing it gently her attention was gradually drawn to a box that has rested on her mantle for a very many years. Looking at it she went over in her mind the contents and was abruptly brought back to the present by a tap on the door and Maggie entering with her tray.

As Elizabeth picked at her food and sipped her tea she went over in her mind any of the conversation she had engaged in while traveling and couldn't really recall anything more than small talk except that she traveled by train from Newcastle. She had obviously come from upper class judging by her dress and manner which also gave the impression of above average schooling. But where are her parents in a time like this? Or, if widowed surely her late husband's family would be willing to care for her and the baby due any time. What would bring her here if there is no family in this area? There seemed too be many questions and no answers, but perhaps tomorrow she would be able to sort a few things out after the young lady has rested. If the baby comes soon as the doctor has indicated it may be necessary to find a nurse that is able to handle the situation. With her thoughts in a jumble she decided to get herself to bed as tomorrow promised to be a busy day. Ringing the bell, she had Maggie bring up a picture of warm water to do her washing and take her tray back to the kitchen. Again she asked how Ms. Grey was doing and Maggie responded, "She seems to be settled in for the night but I will check on her again before I turn in and will check on her a couple of times through the night." With a nod she was dismissed and Elizabeth tucked herself into bed, put out the flame that had cast a soft glow about the room from its lantern and dozed off to sleep.

Morning seemed to come too soon but the house was a buzz with activity. Ellen Blackwell the senior house maid was back. Ellen is slightly older than Elizabeth with hair just starting to show signs of turning silver. Her eyes are a hazel color; she has a straight nose and thin lips. Although her features are sharp she has a kind face which seemed to work well with controlling the younger staff. She is very dedicated to Elizabeth and has been caring for her since Elizabeth had been brought to this house as a new bride. She had been off visiting family while Lady Elizabeth was away visiting her ailing older sister Martha. The cook Mrs. Whitfield was busy preparing breakfast and Maggie was seeing to the needs of Ashley. As Elizabeth entered the main floor she asked Ellen to join her in the study to inform her of the situation they were now facing. Closing the door behind them Elizabeth took a seat behind the desk and motioned for Ellen to take a seat as well.

"I imagine you've already heard we have a guest in the house. I am going to assign Maggie to care for Ashley as they are probably close in age and will probably get along well. I may need to hire a nurse but I will talk to Dr. Denley about it before I go that far. What I would like you to do is open up the nursery and have it dusted and ready. It appears we may have a baby in the house for the first time since my late husband was born here."

"Will you be alright with that Mam? It may be difficult for you to deal with."

"You have been with me long enough to know my pains but you also know I am strong. Perhaps it will be a good thing. As long as the baby lives—let's pray the baby lives. The doctor should be by the house today to see to Ashley and from there maybe we'll understand the situation a little more. If you are finding it too difficult without Maggie's help just let me know and we can look at taking on someone else to help you." With that they left the room and Elizabeth set herself at the table for breakfast.

Maggie's face beamed when she was given the task of looking after Ashley. She had only been with this house for a little better than a year and she respected and admired Lady Elizabeth and the staff were all like one big happy family. Maggie hadn't been part of a family in a long time and the extra responsibility made her feel her position here was secured. Elizabeth then asked how Ms. Grey had slept during the night and Maggie informed her of the troubled night she seamed to have. "She tossed about and she must have been having a bad dream. She kept calling out the name 'William'."

Ashley could hear the sound of a horse and cart coming toward the house and guessed it would be the doctor, as he had said he would be by today. This was confirmed when she heard Maggie talking to the doctor on the way up the stairs. She smoothed the blankets over her swelled belly and tucked her long hair loosely behind her ears. She was very pretty, her hair a nice soft brown with a bouncy curl and at present somewhat tousled from the nights sleep. Her face a little on the pale side compared to normal. She had big brown eyes that seemed to hold a sadness that made her look so vulnerable.

Maggie opened the door to allow Elizabeth and the doctor to enter and both walked over to the bed. "So how is our patient doing today? Did you rest like I told you too?" I nodded, and then winced a bit. "I am getting uncomfortable just lying here but everyone here is extremely kind and I don't think they would allow me to get up even if I wanted to."

"Good, that means they are following my instructions. Let's have a listen to you and your baby." With that Elizabeth stepped back a bit to give the doctor some room as he took out his stethoscope and put it to her chest to listen. Then he pulled the blankets back and gently placed it on her belly to listen. Ashley winced again and the doctor took notice of it. Putting the stethoscope back in his bag he began to gently feel her belly. Then he frowned and felt a little lower. Pulling the blankets back up and tucking them in he asked, "How long have you been getting those pains for?"

"I think about an hour ago. I'm sure it's just from lying around though. It isn't anything regular." She winced again and rubbed her belly. "I can't have the baby yet. It's too soon. I have so much to do; I need to find a place and get some things ready and…" At that the doctor hushed her words and in a kindly but stern voice he cautioned her, not to get excited. "Lady Elizabeth has said you may stay here. To be getting up and about in your condition would definitely not be in the best interests for you or your baby. You may not have much say in this matter. A person doesn't usually get to decide when to go into labor. Your body and the baby have there own timetable, you may already be in mild labor."

Turning to Elizabeth he asked who was going to be tending to her needs. "Ashley needs to be kept calm and rested." At this Maggie was called into the room and the doctor gave her strict instructions to keep her calm and sit with her as much as possible. Turning again to Ashley and in a serious voice he asked her to promise to be good and the rest was crucial. "I'll check back this afternoon. I have a couple of calls I must make." Watching her wince again he turned and made his way to the door and asked if he might have a word with Maggie. Down the stairs and away from earshot he turned to Maggie and asked that she watch for any increasing signs of pain or if they start to come in regular intervals. At that Maggie headed for the stairs to sit with Ashley and Elizabeth came down to have a word with the doctor.

Standing out on the porch it is a beautiful spring day and Elizabeth is looking forward to a stroll in the garden after the doctor leaves but is thinking this might not happen today. Turning to the doctor, and in a concerned voice asks, "Do you think I should hire a nurse in case the baby comes before you can get here, especially if the baby is coming early?"

"That might be wise. I know of a nurse that might just be interested in the short time position. Her name is Margaret Golde. If she is interested I will have her come with me this afternoon. I best be on my way if I am to get things arranged and make it to the other calls and back again." At that he climbed up into his small open carriage and directed the horse down the drive and through the fancy iron gates.

Elizabeth did take a few moments to stroll through the garden and clear her head. She didn't think that young lady looked too good when they met on the train. She was rather pale and looked to be in quite a bit of discomfort. She had no idea the situation was going to change her life forever. But being the person she is she just could not leave that young lady there by herself and it had become apparent nobody was there to meet her.

The idea of a baby in the house brought back memories she had thought she had long buried. Her own two pregnancies ended in tragic still births. Not being able to conceive after that had left her aching in a way that was impossible to describe. Now the memories were all flooding back; the box on her mantle with two small silver cups engraved with the dates of the birth of each baby and two silver spoons. She was going to have to get a hold on her emotions and face the idea of having someone else's baby in the house after giving up the idea so many years ago. This young lady was going to need a lot of help and at least she was in a financial position to give her that.

With emotions now in check again Elizabeth returned to the house. It was time to have a talk to Ashley, and not just small talk. As she entered the house she just caught sight of the back of Maggie heading into the kitchen. "Probably going to get lunch for Ashley and herself" she thought. She has never regretted hiring Maggie. Even though she was orphaned from a very young age, she wasn't bitter and she was so willing to work. She was always smiling even when the cook asked her to scrub pots. She was a little over weight but it tended to suit her. She had beautiful green eyes and just a small spatter of freckles across her nose. She had a small mouth but you never really noticed because the smile always made it look a little bit bigger. As Elizabeth watched Maggie disappear she headed up the stairs. Maggie had left Ashley's door open so Elizabeth just tapped lightly on it and walked in. Ashley looked as though she was deep in thought before she turned her attention towards Elizabeth.

Ashley quickly wiping her eyes, now turned her head to fully face Elizabeth. In a week voice she apologetically started, "I can't thank you enough; your kindness is more than I can ever repay. This is definitely not how I planned things to work out. I should have been booked into a hotel by now and definitely not in labor already. It's too soon. I thought I would have more time to get things together and get some things sorted out."

"Well if you want to repay me, you can do so by taking care to rest. Don't get yourself all worked up. Doing so will not make the situation you're in any better."

"I guess you're wondering what I would be thinking; to travel in my condition and under the circumstances I do owe you an explanation. I would like to ask you though to keep it between you and me."

"I am curious, yes. And if you confide in me, you have my word, I'll not tell anyone."

Between the light contractions she was having she began, "I actually began my travels long before I met you in Birmingham. I think I told you I boarded the train in Newcastle and leaving there was the hardest part for very different reasons than you can imagine. You see, my husband William and I were newly married and we went to Newcastle so I could meet his parents. When we arrived we found his mother to be in quite a state, keeping to her sleeping chambers for hours on end. William's Father had disinherited the youngest son and refused to reconcile their differences. Quite a yelling match happened between William and his father. William tried to get his father to reason on things but it didn't go well at all. His mother heard the yelling match and became even more devastated. She hadn't heard from him in over to a year and didn't even know where he had disappeared to.

It was decided between William and I that William would leave me there to try to coax her out of her room, and he would see if he could locate his brother without his father's knowledge. He told his father he had some business he had to take care of. He headed to Oxford where his brother had finished his education and tried to follow his trail; if he left one. One month later we got a message that my husband had been attacked, robbed and badly beaten. He died from the injuries he received. That sent his mother over the edge and when she began to recover from that news she began to obsess over the upbringing of my baby as if it were somehow to replace William. As the months passed the more possessive she became, and watched my every move. I felt suffocated. I was frightened by the situation and I had to get away. In the last telegram I received before William's death he told me he was looking in Harwell and that is why I chose to come here. This was the last place William was. I…" At this she was cut off by a tap on the door and Maggie entered with a tray of lunch and some tea.

Elizabeth now looked down into Ashley's face and realized she was looking to be in more discomfort and upset from talking about what she had been through. She decided that was enough talk for a bit and excused herself from the room to allow Maggie to tend to her. "Eat something and try to get some rest. We can finish our discussion later. I'll see how you're doing after lunch."

Going from there to across the hall where the nursery is she wanted to check on Ellen's progress. She was busy working away. She had removed all the sheets that covered the furniture, opened up the curtains and was now in the process of washing the large window. Elizabeth was sure her heart skipped a beat or two and she had a lump in her throat. She swallowed hard and realized she would have to get over this feeling. Perhaps having a baby in this room would help. Walking into the center of the room she stood taking it all in. The basinet, the rocking horse in the corner, a chest of drawers possibly still containing the small crisp white gowns she had bought in preparation and a few other bits and pieces, and what nursery would be complete without a rocking chair. Ellen now came and stood beside her. "I took the liberty of removing the clothes from the drawers to have them put in storage. Other than that I think this room is ready."

"It looks nice but have the gowns washed and returned to the drawers. They'll be no good before long and they are nice ones," she paused, "they should be used."

Ellen smoothed her apron down and smiled at what she had accomplished. "Well I've worked up an appetite and I'm finished in here for now. I'm going to the kitchen to see if there is anything left to eat or if Maggie beat me to it. Shall I have a tray done up for you as well?"

"That would be lovely, thank-you."

2
It's a Girl

After going through that day and night with the contractions more intense Ashley was becoming visibly exhausted from the constant pain and lack of sleep. By 3:30 the following afternoon Maggie was beginning to notice a change and headed for the stairs.

Elizabeth was heading up the stairs to check on Ashley at the same time and met halfway. "I was just on my way to get you Mam. Ashley is getting the cramps more steady now and they seem to be increasing in strength. Is the doctor expected to be by soon?"

"I would think so. I'll check on her and please send Ellen up. She has helped deliver a baby or two in her time. She might know what to do to alleviate some of her discomfort." On those words they both continued in the directions they were headed.

Elizabeth entered Ashley's room and Ellen was not far behind. Ashley was hugging a pillow tightly and after a few seconds passed she relaxed. Elizabeth took a cloth from a water basin and wrung it out. She dabbed Ashley's face with it and laid it across her forehead. "How far apart are the contractions?"

"Probably 15 minutes but they are consistent, and they hurt. They're much stronger than when Dr. Denley was here earlier. Is he going to come by later today?"

"I expect him anytime."

Now Ellen added to the conversation. "You still have a ways to go. If your contractions get to 5 to 10 minutes apart and the doctor hasn't arrived it would definitely be time to send someone for him. The best thing you can do is try to rest between as much as possible."

Dr. Denley came at 4:00 with Margaret Golde. Maggie took her bags for her and Ellen led them to Ashley's room. Elizabeth filled them in on what was happening and Dr. Denley asked all but the nurse to leave the room while he washed his hands and examined her carefully. It was very uncomfortable to have this good-looking young doctor checking her like that but she was at his mercy. By the time he was finished Ashley was sure she must be blushing and kept her face looking down at the blankets as he was pulling them back up and tucking them in a bit. Then he pulled the chair around to sit facing her, obviously he had something important to tell her by the expression on his face. "When I checked you earlier today and felt your belly I was trying to figure out the position of the baby and I was worried we might be faced with a breach baby. That's when the baby comes feet first, instead of head and I believe that is the baby's position. It's a more difficult delivery but I have delivered a few. You can get through this. Mrs. Golde has helped me deliver a couple of babies in the breach position and she will be directing you. Just follow the directions given. That is extremely important. I can't emphasize that enough."

Ashley's lips quivered but she was not going to cry…or at least try not to show it. She quickly put her hand to her mouth.

Dr. Denley grabbed her other hand in his and in a reassuring voice said, "I know you're scared, but it'll be ok.

By 6:30 Ashley's water broke and the contractions intensified even more and started lasting longer. They started to come so close together that it didn't seem like there was any time between. It was time to bear down and push. With Elizabeth on one side of Ashley and Maggie on the other, Ashley was gripping their hands and clenching her teeth. Dr. Denley all the while was telling her she was doing good. Then Ashley could feel the baby coming out and Dr. Denley told her it was very important now to push as hard as she could. "We want the head out quickly because your baby's air supply will be cut off because of the pressure on the umbilical cord. Now PUSH, PUSH, PUSH and again PUSH. You're doing good...One more time, now push, PUSH for all your worth!"

Ashley let out a scream and the baby was out and that's all she remembered. She was completely and totally exhausted. The cord was tied and cut and a very tiny baby was handed over to the nurse to make sure it was breathing while the doctor tended to Ashley. What he hadn't counted on was the extreme amount of blood that followed. Fighting to get that under control Maggie rushed out of the room in tears and headed to the kitchen to get the blankets that the cook was keeping warm for them.

Dr. Denley and Elizabeth sat one on each side of Ashley waiting for her to wake up. Margaret Golde and Ellen were fusing over the baby, cleaning it up, and making sure it was breathing.

"I want the baby left in this room so Ashley can hear it cry. It will give her a reason to fight. She is going to be really weak and will need plenty of rest and around the clock care."

At 10:00 PM. Ashley's eyes fluttered open long enough to realize it was all over. "My baby, is it alright?" Margaret brought the baby over and within inches from her face, "meet your little baby girl." A weak smile passed on Ashley's pale face and she was out again.

Maggie showed Margaret to a small room off the nursery and then headed off to bed. Dr. Denley encouraged Ellen and

Elizabeth to get some rest as well. "I'm going to sit here through the night to keep checking on Ashley. I want to make sure the bleeding doesn't start up again and Margaret will be tending the baby as needed."

Dr. Denley left the next morning after examining Ashley and her little baby girl and faithfully checked on them both twice a day for the next four days. Her baby was extremely tiny and would need some special care. It was a good thing Margaret Golde had accepted the position here.

Elizabeth made Ashley's room her first stop each morning to check on both before going down to breakfast. She had the rocking chair moved from the nursery to Ashley's room and made a habit of spending hours rocking the baby, quite content. She kept telling herself not to get too attached but could not help herself. This was something she was never privileged to do with her own two babies. She was going to enjoy this for as long as it lasted and when it was time for them to leave she knew she would be saddened but she also knew she would grieve for the babies she had lost all over again but she wasn't going to miss this opportunity.

Slowly you could see Ashley's color improving and her strength increasing. By the end of a week she was sitting up and taking care of some of her baby's needs and Elizabeth was right there to help with anything else. "I have been thinking of a name for my baby. I want to name her after my mother but if you would permit me I would like to include your name as well. I would like to name her Katlaina Elizabeth. I know it seems like a big name for such a tiny baby but we can call her Katie until she grows into it. You have been so kind; I don't know what I would have done if you hadn't been on the coach with me that day. I want Katie to grow up knowing how she came to have her second name Elizabeth." With that Elizabeth's eyes brimmed with tears and she was only able to give a nod for the lump in her throat. This little baby girl that she had grown so attached to was going to carry her name.

Dr. Denley was now checking on Ashley in the mornings and at the end of two weeks it was no longer necessary to keep Margaret Gold on. As tiny as Katie was she was finally holding her own and starting to gain a little weight. Ashley hadn't been given permission to be up and about yet so she asked Maggie to go into her trunk and find a small purse. Margaret would be leaving soon and Ashley wanted to pay her for all the care she and her baby had received.

"I cannot accept that. Lady Elizabeth has already taken care of it, and she has been very generous. Before I leave I want to let you know you are a very good patient and I wanted to wish you and your baby Katie the best. Perhaps we'll meet again sometime and hopefully under better conditions."

As Ashley watched her leave, Dr. Denley came in and this time took the chair by her bed and turned it to face her. The last time he did that he had bad news.

Ashley wasn't prepared for what he had to tell her.

"You know you bled a lot and gave us all a really big scare. There were other complications during the delivery and I hope I'm wrong, but you may not be able to have any more babies. I'm so sorry; I wish it would have been better news for you."

Ashley was numb; she didn't know what to think. She no longer had a husband and was not sure she would ever love anyone else. But what if she did find someone special again? What if he wanted children of his own?

"I know it's a lot to take in, so I want you to rest today but starting tomorrow I want you to start getting up and about a bit. Don't over do it but gradually work up to a normal routine. I'll check on you again in a couple of days."

As he was leaving Maggie came in and noticing the shocked look in Ashley's eyes she dashed out again. She spoke a couple of words to Elizabeth and headed for the kitchen. Maggie returned with two cups of tea on a tray with a few treats and as she was encouraging her to have a cup of tea Elizabeth entered the room. Maggie asked if she could take Katie out for a bath and a change and with permission granted she picked her up like she would break if handled too much and out she went cooing and talking to her as she went.

"I want to thank you for hiring Mrs. Golde but I can pay you for that.'

"That won't be necessary. I hired Margaret Golde without consulting you so I feel it is my obligation to pay. It's done. You know that is not why I came in here though, don't you?"

"Yes, I have a feeling Maggie has talked to you, I'm fine though. Dr. Denley just told me I may not be able to have any more babies and I guess Maggie told you I looked a bit shocked when he left, but I'm Ok."

"Well we won't dwell on the negative, may be he is wrong."

"He said he hoped he was wrong but just the way he said it and the expression on his face; I don't think he believes that to be the case. He said there were other complications."

"You have a beautiful little baby girl to tend to and I suggest you enjoy every precious moment you can with her. Now for some good news Dr. Denley told me I'm to get you up and about a bit tomorrow. I was thinking you might join me downstairs for tea and take a small stroll around the grounds. It might be nice for you see a bit more of the house than these four walls you've been looking at. A bit of scenery change and some fresh air might be good for you. It will be nice to get you out of these night gowns as well."

"I will look forward to that." They sipped their tea and enjoyed small talk about the flowers in the garden and how warm the spring has been.

Two days later Dr. Denley returned to check on Ashley and found her and Elizabeth walking around the garden enjoying the spring flowers that had been appearing. He was accompanied by a very well dressed young lady he introduced as his fiancé. She was wearing an emerald green floor length dress of satin with matching hat and gloves. Her hair was done up under the hat with small wisps falling out around her face. She had a beautiful complexion with hazel eyes and a little turned up nose that seemed to suite her face. "I hope you don't mind her presence here. Sarah wanted to come on the rounds with me today to see what it's like and is quite likely to be accompanying me on a lot of my house calls after we are married."

Ashley gave a small nod, "I'm pleased to meet you and may I offer my congratulations. Have you set your date yet?"

"Hopefully this summer; though I have yet to meet some of his family."

Dr. Denley quickly excused himself and said he should check little Katie over and Ashley led him up to the nursery. At just over two weeks old Katie had gained a bit more weight but was still so tiny. "She is healthy but I would be happier if she was a little bigger. Bring her by the office in a few weeks just so I can check on her progress. And how have you been feeling? You're color is improving and you're looking better each time I see you."

"I feel like I'm getting back to my usual self again."

"How are you dealing with what I told you last time I was by?"

"I'm still a little numb about the whole idea but I have no husband and it may never matter so I'll deal with it later if I have to."

"Well by the look of things you can return to a regular routine as your energy permits but again—do not over do it or tire yourself out. Katie needs you strong and healthy."

Ashley scooped Katie up wrapping a cozy blanket around her and led the way out of the nursery and back out to the garden where they had left Elizabeth and Sarah talking.

Dr. Denley could see Elizabeth's eyes light up when she caught sight of Katie and how she automatically reached out to take her from Ashley. With the mention of more calls to make and a "good-bye" Dr. Denley helped Sarah up into the buggy, climbed up beside her and gave the reigns a little flick. The horse lifted her head and hooves into motion she trotted down the drive.

Over the next few days Ashley was improving in great strides and was beginning to think it was time to find a place of her own and pay her farewells. She started checking the papers for anything available and was not succeeding in finding anything suitable. Two weeks went by and she decided to look around again when she took Katie for her check-up. She had a couple of letters to send out. One to a friend, Josie, she hadn't seen in some time and she had so much to tell her since they last spoke. If nothing else she wanted to let her know where she was these days.

Elizabeth decided to join her for the ride and thought a bit of shopping would make for a nice outing. She really would like to see the new fabrics and lace the shops brought in for spring and have a new dress made. Ashley hadn't been able to check out the town when she arrived and Elizabeth knew of the best places to shop. The smells coming from the bakery made her hungry, people were buzzing around in a flurry of activity and there were people selling their baskets and cut flowers, pottery and other wares; it felt so good just to be out again. They chatted amiably while they took turns pushing the baby carriage and most people observing them would have thought them to be mother and daughter or at least very good friends. There was a comfortableness between them that just seemed so natural.

With very little coaxing from Elizabeth they entered an elegant little restaurant that was Elizabeth's favorite spot when she came to town. The head waitress smiled widely and exclaimed her pleasure at seeing her. "It's been a while. I trust your trip was fine and your sister is improving?"

"Yes everything went well, thank-you."

"I have a nice table for you overlooking the pond. Would you like the usual or would you like a menu today?"

"I think menus would be a good idea and I would like to introduce you to my guest. This is Ashley Grey and her baby Katie." Seating themselves at the table the waitress disappeared and quickly returned with a pot of tea and menus.

It was time to let Elizabeth know of her intentions. "I have been looking for a suitable home to rent and unfortunately I am not seeing too much available but I promise to be out of your way as soon as possible. If you want me out sooner I can take up a room at a Hotel. That was my original idea before I blacked out at the station."

With a wave of her hand and taking a deep breath Elizabeth began, "I have no intentions of having you move into a hotel. I quite enjoy having you and Katie at the house. I would like it very much if you would stay and make it your home for as long as you want. I enjoy the company and truth be told I would miss you and Katie very much if you left now. If you are determined to find a place of your own though I'll help in any way I can, and if that is your decision I would still dearly love to have you visit and keep in touch. I don't expect an answer right away. I realize it's something you will want to think over and if you think of anything you need to know before making a decision, don't hesitate to ask. With that said we should probably order. I'm treating and sandwiches are always good here if that's alright with you."

Ashley smiled and nodded, and the proposition Elizabeth just made sounded good and she would definitely consider it.

Katie's check-up went fine and the rest of the afternoon was spent just looking at the different shops of interest before heading back to what Ashley was now starting to consider as home.

Ashley began to look forward to their regular morning strolls through the garden and took the opportunity one morning to let Elizabeth know that if the offer still stood she would be happy to remain here for now. "I do love it here and it would be a shame to uproot Katie at this point. Maggie is very attentive and helpful with her, and I do believe you have a soft spot for Katie as well. This does feel like home for me too."

3
Meeting Clive

    Clive walked in unannounced as he sometimes does and immediately tried to demand attention. Maggie did not rush to the door to greet him and Elizabeth and Ashley had gone to town for a much needed outing. Ellen Blackwell went to the entrance to see who had entered half expecting to receive greetings from Elizabeth and Ashley and prepared to take parcels up stairs for them only to be harshly demanded to take Clive's carpet bag up to his usual room. "What is that terrible noise coming from upstairs? Is that a BABY I hear? Has everyone gone mad in this house? I demand an explanation!"

    Clive is Elizabeth's only nephew and apart from her sister Martha, he is the only living relative. At 5'11", Clive is impeccably dressed with almost black hair, steely eyes, a long straight nose and a neatly kept mustache. There seemed to be a dark side to him that he kept well hidden. He expected nothing less than a proper greeting and for house maids to speak only when spoken to.

    Reaching out for the carpet bag Ellen politely told him that Elizabeth would be home shortly. "It is a baby you hear and you might wish to have a different room this evening. Lady Elizabeth will explain everything when she arrives. Would you care for a drink in the study?"

Looking not a little disturbed he said he would be quite capable of pouring a drink for himself as he strode into the study.

Rushing up the stairs Ellen headed for the nursery where Maggie was trying desperately to calm a very cranky little Katie. "She may be tiny but she has really good lungs."

"I just wanted to warn you that Clive has just arrived so you can be perfectly proper when you go down stairs. Do you think a bottle would calm Katie?"

"No. Ashley said she would be back home in time to nurse her and that should be any time now. I'll try to hold her off a bit longer."

At that Ellen rushed out of the nursery and headed down to the kitchen to inform the cook to prepare a tray for Clive and that he most likely would be dining with Elizabeth and Ashley. With a couple of scones, fresh butter and a couple of sweets placed on a tray Ellen took it into Clive. With a small nod she left and headed out the front door and onto the porch. She was always a bundle of nerves every time he came. He was very intimidating and it was easy to slip up because of the friendlier, family type atmosphere that was the norm in this house. She slipped up once by calling him by his given name and she was tongue lashed for doing so. Had he had his way he would have fired her on the spot. She had determined never to make that mistake again.

Standing on the porch she peered down the drive trying to look through the trees but they were filling in with leaves and the beautiful colors of spring so well she couldn't see too far. But the faint sound of hooves trotting up the drive told her they would be in sight in a mater of seconds. Lady Elizabeth had changed so much since Ashley had told her she would accept the offer to stay. She had become happier and livelier. She needed a heads up about the presence of Clive before walking in. After the warning Ellen gathered up the parcels and took them in, giving Elizabeth a chance to explain to Ashley who he is and how the way they talk to Maggie and Ellen would have to be very proper.

From what Elizabeth told her, she didn't think she was going to like Clive being here, but it was Elizabeth's nephew so she needed to be polite. Heading into the house Ashley hurried up the stairs to the nursery where poor Maggie was still trying to calm Katie. "Oh Maggie I am so sorry. I hope she hasn't been like this for too long. If this ever happens again you go ahead and feed her. It's not your responsibility to tend to a screaming baby." Taking Katie in her arms she quickly changed the screaming to a content little baby.

"I knew you would be back any time. Please excuse me. I have to go prepare a different room for Cli…I mean Master Dane. He will not want to sleep too close to the nursery with Katie waking up every few hours." She left the room and Ashley sat nursing Katie and soothing her with a soft motherly voice. When she was finished feeding her a change was in order and then Ashley wanted to freshen up before meeting Elizabeth's nephew.

Finally ready and carrying Katie over her shoulder she headed down the stairs and towards the sitting room. Caught off guard she was abruptly confronted by Clive who seemed to have a disapproving look in his eyes. "I presume you are Ashley Grey, my aunt has been telling me about you and obviously this is the baby that was making all the noise. No doubt you have already been told my name is Clive Dane." At that he held out his hand in greeting. Looking at her she was very beautiful in appearance. Her hair was loosely piled on her head. She was wearing a light pink floor length dress with some embroidery on the collar, soft pleats, and buttons down the front. She offered her hand back in greeting, "It's very nice to meet you," then excused herself and continued on her way to the sitting room.

"Clive has just gone to wash up and then he will join us. You have no doubt already met on your way down but we can have a drink and it will give you a chance to get to know him a bit before dinner."

Maggie entered the room and offered to take Katie but was denied. "I feel like I have neglected her too much already today so I'll hold her a little longer and you can take her at dinner time if that's alright." Maggie responded back in a curt voice, "Yes Mam," that made Ashley feel uncomfortable and felt she had maybe slighted her until she realized that Clive was standing directly behind her.

Elizabeth monopolized the conversation so Ashley could jump in when she felt comfortable. "How's your mother doing? She was in rough shape last I saw her. It was on the coach ride home that I happened to meet Ashley. She has been a god send, bringing this house back to life."

"Mother is still making improvements but the worst is over. Speaking of god sends, why haven't you employed a butler so your guests can be properly met at the door upon arrival? It was disgraceful when I walked in this afternoon."

"We've been over this before. I have no need of a butler. I hired Maggie not as a butler but to help take up the slack."

"Yes, well Maggie did not greet me at the door to take my coat and bags."

"She was obviously busy tending to Katie but Ellen was here and she is more that qualified to tend to your needs upon arrival."

"Well maybe consider a nanny. Are babies not usually tended to in a nursery?"

"Clive you are not in a position to take over my decisions of how I run my house. I am still able to make decisions and this home is running quite nicely. Maggie has been given the duty of seeing to Ashley and the baby and she is good at it. I have told

Ellen if the work load becomes too much for her I will hire someone else to help but so far she is managing quite nicely. If you want a butler bring yours with you when you come. As for Katie being out of the nursery, she is out quite often and we are all enjoying her presence very much. I think we should change the subject now and head to the dining room. Mrs. Whitfield has prepared lamb and I do believe it is about ready."

At that they headed for the dining room and enjoyed a more pleasant conversation than they had in the sitting room. Ashley headed up early to tend to Katie and get her tucked in and decided on an early night herself. She really didn't care to be in the company of Clive.

When she finally woke in the morning and went down Clive made a point of looking at his watch. Pity the poor woman that ever marries him she thought to herself. "I'm sorry for being so late. Katie kept me up a lot during the night. She is running a bit of a fever. I think I'll take her to town and have Dr. Denley take a look at her."

"Clive is heading out at noon. If it's ok with you Ashley, we can take him as far as the station, unless you were wanting some time on your own."

"No that will be fine; it looks like it's going to be a lovely day. I'll have a bite to eat and go get ready. Perhaps Maggie would like the outing too." She said that more to get a rise out of Clive than anything and Elizabeth knew it. She also knew there would be no way Clive would travel in the same buggy as Maggie.

"I'll give Maggie the rest of the morning off and she can go early and run her personal errands. She can meet up with us for the ride back."

Clive sat quietly listening to the two not really believing how changed his Aunt has been this visit and wondering if Ashley was going to be a threat to his inheriting this place eventually. He was obviously going to be keeping close watch on the situation and start thinking of possible damage control.

Dr. Denley wasn't in the clinic when they first arrived so Elizabeth offered to buy Ashley lunch at her favorite place before they headed back to Dr. Denley's office. Dr. Denley and Sarah passed the window they were seated at probably heading for the office after doing some house calls, but Sarah didn't look too pleased. Dr. Denley wasn't exactly smiling either. Ashley remembered those types of moments when she and William had disagreements. Oh how she missed him, and he would have loved his little girl.

"Ashley are you alright; the waitress is waiting for your order."

"Oh, I'm so sorry. I was lost in thought." Apologizing, she placed her order and tried to keep up with the conversation. By the time they got to Dr. Denley's office, he and Sarah were smiling again and Ashley thought she might have just imagined things.

"Katie seems fine. It was probably nothing to be concerned about. I am pleased with her weight now. She's just over a month old and doing well."

The rest of their afternoon went pretty much as planned. Maggie met up with them carrying a couple of parcels and was happy for the ride back. Ashley and Maggie had become good friends and they were good for each other. Maggie even looked as if she was slimming down a bit, probably from all the trips up and down the stairs. But Elizabeth noticed she was looking good.

A few months seemed to go by and Elizabeth got involved again in some of the charity work she had done before going to Martha's and then having Ashley in her home she had become quite consumed with Katie and Ashley. Summer was slowly slipping away and it was a particularly hot day in August when news came of a huge explosion at the local coal mine on the outskirts of town. Men and young boys and girls were buried and residents were desperately digging, hoping to find them alive. Wives and family members huddled together hoping of good news.

Elizabeth and Ashley decided to go see if there was anything they could do to help and Maggie stayed behind to care for Katie. The dust hung heavy in the air and with the added heat there was a smell lingering that a person would never forget. It was a terrible sight at the mine. Ashley had never been there before. Women were clutching the hands of their little ones and crying because they didn't know if their husband, sons or daughters would be brought out alive. The waiting seemed to last an eternity as they were trying to organize the men in groups so they could take turns digging. Each time someone was brought out Dr. Denley pronounced him dead, the name was posted and more wailing was heard.

Elizabeth donated refreshments to be brought for the men tirelessly working at digging out the bodies in hopeful search of the living, and Ashley tried to console those waiting for word.

The heat must have been almost unbearable for those trying to do the digging and with everything being so unstable inside it was taking longer as they had to reinforce some areas before they could safely attempt a rescue. The fear of more walls collapsing was ever present on their minds. They worked in shifts with some of them refusing to stop until everyone was out.

Their faces black from the grime and sweat the first person to be brought out alive was a young boy of about 11 years old and a cheer followed as Dr. Denley began looking him over and treating some bad cuts. Ashley rushed over to give him a hand as the boy was thrashing around and they needed to get the cuts cleaned. She realized then that Sarah his fiancée and helper was nowhere to be seen. Another was brought out alive and Dr.

Denley required assistance and so Ashley worked along with him taking orders and helping as much as she was able. They worked together on cuts, bruises, broken bones and dislocated shoulders. They worked tirelessly for hours until Dr. Denley finally had a grip on things and sent Ashley home for a well needed sleep and realizing she must have been about desperate to nurse Katie.

Ashley looked around and realized Elizabeth would have been long gone and Dr. Denley kindly told her to take his horse and cart and he would send for them later.

Back at home Maggie had a bath prepared for her and she quickly washed up and nursed Katie much to her relief. By the time she crawled into bed she was exhausted but Maggie told her not to worry. She would listen for Katie and take care of her. She slept till 6 AM and woke with a start. She heard Katie and quickly got up to nurse her and check to see if Maggie had heard any more news.

Maggie brought in a breakfast tray for Ashley to eat while nursing Katie and told her Elizabeth was getting ready to head back to the mine.

"When I'm ready I'll go back too if you can watch over Katie again."

"That will be fine, I love taking care of her."

By the time she was heading back out to the mine with Dr. Denley's horse and cart she had at least felt somewhat rested. She relieved Elizabeth who was helping the Doctor and they worked again as more dead and injured were brought out. Some of the injuries were terrible to look at because of being dug out from under heavy rock and wooden beams. Finally the last unaccounted person was brought out. The crowds began to disperse. Some were taking their injured loved ones home with them while others were going home feeling the loss of a loved one and yet there were others knowing their loved ones would be at the hospital for further treatment. Finally the last one was being strapped onto a cart to be taken to the hospital for stitches. They washed their hands in silence at a basin provided. "I see you brought my horse and cart back. I can at least offer you a ride home."

She accepted his hand as he helped her into the cart and watched him climb up on the other side. He must be extremely exhausted. He had worked straight through catching a little nap between patients here and there. He gave the reigns a little flick, the cart gave a jerk and off they were, heading towards home.

Pulling the horse to a halt at the entrance he turned to Ashley and looking at her he brushed his index finger gently against her cheek wiping a black smudge off. "Thank-you so much for all your help, I don't know how I would have managed without it. Please thank Elizabeth for me for all her help as well. I really have to get to the hospital now." He hopped down, walked around the cart to help her down and made sure she was safely in the door before he left. Maggie again had a bath prepared for Ashley and told her this time she had time for a soak if she wanted because she had just finished feeding Katie not an hour ago. To Ashley that sounded so good. She almost fell asleep in the tub. Finally when she climbed out and wrapped in her robe she tip toed to her room and collapsed in bed still wrapped in her robe. Two hours later she heard Katie and headed for the nursery and almost walked straight into Maggie. "I thought I would bring her to you so you could nurse her and then I'll take care of her so you can get more sleep."

"Thank-you so much; you are such a dear." Nursing Katie and talking softly to her all she could think of was how Dr. Denley had wiped the black smudge off her cheek before helping her down, and the feel of his hand. She had no right to think like that, he was an engaged man and she had only been widowed 9 months. It was probably just that she missed the little things about William. How he would take her hand or brush a piece of hair out of her face. She handed Katie back to Maggie and sunk back down in her bed. Maggie brought her in a sandwich and a cup of tea encouraging her to eat it before falling asleep.

"Please don't let me sleep through dinner or I'll never sleep tonight." With those words she was out. Katie didn't let her sleep that long though and as tired as she was still it was Katie that came first and she was demanding attention in a very strong way. It wasn't time for a feeding so she gathered her up into her arms and carried her downstairs. She had barely seen anything of Elizabeth since the explosion and she wanted to see if she had been getting rested up. They had tea together on the porch and discussed the needs of the ones who were affected by the mine and what they could do to ease their pain.

Ashley enjoyed helping others as it helped her forget about her own problems. There was that ever nagging fear that William's parents would be looking for her. By now they would know she will have had her baby and they may want to take control of things to have that small part of William back. Elizabeth had taken Katie as she often did

and was bouncing her up and down while they discussed things. "I have missed our morning walks in the garden the last few days but things will get back to normal now."

Dr Denley arrived back at his small place. Totally exhausted, he cleaned up and slept for a good twelve hours straight. When he finally woke up he still felt tired but it would probably take a few days to feel normal again. He looked at a note he had set on the table some time ago and shook his head. Why had he not seen what had been happening? There were signs that it wasn't going to work but he refused to see them. She enjoyed going on the house calls to the big fancy homes but she deplored going down the dirty streets where the homes were nothing more than shacks. Little children with dirty faces going bare foot barely having enough to eat let alone having much more than rags to wear. While he felt empathy for them she seemed to look down her nose at them.

   Gradually her attitude became worse but he looked the other way and figured as time went on she would come around. After all, they were in love and didn't loved ones make adjustment to try and please the one they love. She knew what was involved before she ever agreed to getting married.

   Then on some of the house calls she barely stepped inside the door but on the last house call she had come with him she refused to get out of the carriage preferring to sit outside no matter how long it was going to take. There was one time he could have really used her help. It wasn't that she didn't know what to do either. She had been trained in nursing skills. He had to deliver a baby that was too big for the tiny unwed mother and just being there to hold her hand for emotional support would have made it so much easier for the young girl. She almost died. The ride back to the clinic that day was especially tense and few words were spoken but you could read the expressions on each of their faces. Her actions said it all.

   Denley was glad for the interruption to the mood with the arrival of Ms. Grey. She had dropped by to have him look at Katie. She was running a slight fever and being a new mother she was a little concerned.

   A few days later he found this note under his door:

Dear Denley:

I am sorry for what I have to say. I know it won't work out though and it is best I go back to my family in London. I can't live the life you want me too. I thought at first I could, but I cannot bring myself to make the changes you were expecting of me and I cannot understand how you can lower yourself to treat those people. I realize they too need medical help but not from me. I should have said this to you in person but I can't face you. I think enough was said and felt the other day. I do wish you the best. Sarah

He folded the paper in half and put it away, out of sight. He really didn't need to read it again. He had it almost memorized.

For some strange reason he thought of Ashley. How she worked with him on those injured in the mine without a hint of distaste. How pretty she looked, even with that black smudge on her cheek.

4
Set Up

Clive showed up the next day as news of the mine started spreading. He knew his Aunt would be involved in relief efforts of some kind. The very idea of her working on those dirty people was repulsive to him but that was her nature and try as he and his mom had, Elizabeth was solid in her decisions. Her late husband had changed her so much and even after his passing she didn't go back to her former self. At least this time he was properly met at the door by Maggie. He stayed two days this time and being his normal self, Ashley did what she could to avoid being in his presence as much as possible. When they were unable to avoid each other Ashley did little things to annoy Clive and Elizabeth had to chuckle to herself at some of her antics. Katie had started teething and was very irritable. She kept everyone on their toes.

Maggie approached Elizabeth privately when Clive had gone to the stables for a ride and she was stewing about something. "I have to tell you something Mam.

It's…well it's about something I saw Master Clive do when I was just coming out of the nursery and he didn't see me," she paused not sure how to go on.

"Well Maggie, if you have something important to tell me, and it is obviously bothering you, you best just say it and you'll feel better."

"It's just that I saw him walking from your room to Ashley's and it looked like he was carrying the necklace you wear on special occasions. But when he came out it didn't look like he was still holding it."

"Maggie are you sure that's what you saw?"

"I'm fairly sure Mam. I don't think he likes Ashley and it probably goes both ways. But your right, I do feel better."

Ok Maggie I'll take care of this. I want you to pretend you didn't see anything or say anything and what ever happens, go along with it."

Maggie was dismissed and Elizabeth headed up the stairs. Tapping gently on the door in case Katie was sleeping, Ashley opened the door to Elizabeth and after accepting a chair that was still by the bed she asked Ashley if a necklace had shown up in her room. "I'm not accusing you of taking it. I think it may have been planted in here." Together they looked and found it tucked under a doily on her chest.

"I don't understand why it would have been put there."

"I know you don't, but I do. When Clive returns from his ride I want you to play along with me and express your innocence in the whole thing. I'll get to the bottom of things." Elizabeth had to inform Ellen of everything and asked her to play along as well.

Elizabeth was confronting Ashley with the necklace in her hand as Clive came in the door. "Ellen found this in your room while she was dusting. I can't believe after all I've done for you that you would steal from me."

"I didn't take it! I don't know how it got to be in my room but you have to believe me. I didn't steal it."

Clive interrupted the conversation now. "You were stealing from my Aunt. I'm sending for the police."

"No Clive I can deal with this thank-you."

"Aunt Elizabeth if she is stealing from you who knows what else she has taken. Her room should be searched completely. That necklace is a very expensive piece of jewelry. They would lock her up and throw away the key."

Clive watched in satisfaction as Ashley turned on the tears and swore she didn't take it. He smiled inwardly when he heard Elizabeth tell her to save her tears. It wasn't going to convince her. The evidence was found hid in her bedroom.

Clive turned to Elizabeth and again he said they should send for the police.

"Perhaps you should send for the police and you can explain to them why YOU put the necklace in Ashley's room. You weren't so discreet. You can go and pack your bags and don't bother to come back. I can't believe you would stoop to such a low thing. You would have been willing to destroy Ashley's life and Katie's and not only that but you entered rooms that you were not permitted access to. How dare you! I wonder what your mother would say."

With no way of explaining it away he turned on his heels leaving the room and left ten minutes later with a slam of the door.

"That boy has been so spoiled. I hope he learns some humility from all this. It will probably be a bit before we see him again. I wouldn't be surprised if you find more of my jewelry and belongings show up in your room Ashley. He indicated the need for it to be thoroughly searched. It almost sounded like he thought we would find more. Thank-you for going along with me, I hope I wasn't too harsh on you."

"We may not have liked each other but I don't understand why he would do such a thing. I'll look through my room tomorrow and see if anything else shows up."

The next morning Ashley went through her room to find a few trinkets and a pair of cufflinks. He was prepared to set her up good. She was absolutely shaken when she realized what would have happened had he succeeded, not only to her but also to Katie. He was dangerous and she didn't know what he was capable of.

She needed to go to the library tomorrow and find the answers she was looking for about William's death and maybe it would help lead her to his brother. At least then if she had to leave she would have what she came for if there's anything to find.

Returning the things to Elizabeth she was shocked to see the depth of Clive's maliciousness. "I'll send these cuff links back to his mother along with a letter of explanation. Would you like to come with me to town? I have some important matters to take care of. If you can amuse yourself for a bit in town we can meet up for tea and crumpets."

"That sounds good and actually I want to check out the library." I think I will see if Maggie will watch Katie. A library is no place to take a fussy baby."

By 1:00 they were headed to town and Ashley was dropped off at the library. It was a nice building. It had large beams on each side of the six steps up to the entrance and walking in, there was a quietness to the library that was calming. There was also the smell of books and this library had an extensive collection. She looked around at the tables and chairs set up and spotted a quiet corner that would be nice.

Going over to the head librarian she asked him if they kept copies of old news papers. "I am looking for ones dated around the first of December to about the middle of January of last year."

With the copies in hand she headed to the corner table and sat down. Flipping pages she scanned them for any news headlines that might reveal information about William. In January's issue she found a column about a man robbed and beaten at the end of December. He was left for dead and as she read further she could feel the blood run from her face. She was sure she must have paled drastically. She found William's name briefly mentioned. Continuing down the column she noticed another name, this was a woman's name and she was apparently the one that found him. Ashley quickly wrote the name Rosie Boyle down and finished reading the column. She was beginning to wish she hadn't found anything because it made her feel so raw again. She would have to look up Rosie and find out if William said anything to her before he died. She folded the paper back up to return it to the head librarian but when she went to stand her legs didn't feel like they were going to hold her up.

She stood for a few seconds holding the table composing herself before she tried to move again. Picking out a book she wanted to read she returned the papers and walked back out. It was probably time to meet up with Elizabeth so she began down the stairs when two boys rushed on her, one grabbing for her purse and pushing her so violently that she hit her head hard on one of the pillars before slamming her head on the steps as she landed. The other boy thrust a knife deep into her side. They ran off disappearing as quickly as they had run in.

People began to run to Ashley's aid and lying unconscious in a pool of blood they immediately sent for a doctor.

Elizabeth had finished her tea and decided to go out and see if there was any sign of Ashley coming. Looking at the commotion down the street at the front of the library she got a sick feeling in her stomach and began to hurry in that direction. Dr. Denley raced by in his carriage and stopped there and grabbing up his medical bag he made his way through the growing crowd. Elizabeth now arrived at the site too. She stood in horror listening to what had happened and seeing Ashley motionless and lying in a pool of blood. Dr. Denley worked quickly and in desperation he tried to contain the bleeding and assess how best to move her. She was strapped onto a board and loaded onto the carriage. Elizabeth climbed up on the one side of her and Dr. Denley on the other. Someone from the gathering group of people jumped into the front and took up the reigns. The trip to the hospital was quick but to Elizabeth they couldn't seem to get there fast enough. Dr. Denley was holding pressure on her side to try to control the bleeding.

Ashley was rushed into the operating room immediately and Dr. Denley worked on her for a number of hours. The stab wound to her side had missed her vital organs but the bleeding was a problem. Once that was contained he had her head injuries to contend with and they appeared to be serious. Along with that she had some other scrapes and cuts on her face and within her hair line. They had to clip hair away to be able to stitch up some of the deeper cuts.

Elizabeth paced the floor in the waiting area until Dr. Denley finally came out of surgery and told her Ashley's condition.

"She was stabbed in the side and has lost a lot of blood but it is her head injuries I am most concerned about now and the threat of infection. We won't know how bad they are until she wakes up and I have no way of knowing how long that will be. She is all bandaged up and when you see her you must remain calm. She also has smaller cuts and bruising appearing on her face but most of the permanent scarring will be concealed when her hair grows back." Watching the panic grow on Elizabeth's face Dr. Denley took her gently by the shoulders and held her while he reinforced the idea of remaining calm. Then giving her a hug he turned her towards the door.

Finally Ashley was wheeled out of the operating room and her bed was placed closest to the nurse's station so she could be watched carefully.

"May I go over and see her?"

"You may, but not for too long and you must remain calm."

Margaret Golde stood by her bed checking her pulse when Elizabeth tip toed over. She stood holding her hand over her mouth to prevent making any noise for a couple of minutes and then was ushered away. Before Elizabeth left the hospital a police man entered and talked to a nurse at the front desk. Elizabeth waited to talk to him and told him who she was and how Ashley was connected to her household. "Do you have any idea what happed, who did this to her?"

"We are working on a few leads and are hoping to talk to this young woman when she wakes up. I have nothing more to tell you at the present, but we'll keep you informed." He went over to talk to Dr. Denley and Elizabeth left. Maggie was going to be wondering what has happened.

Elizabeth arrived home and headed straight for the study. She didn't drink too often but she needed one now. The last week has been a nightmare but today was a nightmare she wanted to wake up from.

Maggie tapped on the study door and when she poked her head in Elizabeth asked her to go and get Ellen. She needed to talk to both of them.

Maggie put her hand over her mouth to try to cover her horror and Ellen sat wringing her hands. "Who could do such a thing?" Not really expecting an answer. Elizabeth watched Maggie's eyes fill with tears as it slowly sunk in. She was especially attached to Ashley.

"Maggie, are you able to care for Katie. It may be some time before Ashley is home and we don't know how long before she can look after her on her own-if ever? If it's too much for you I can hire a nanny."

No nanny, please Mam. I'll take care of Katie. Ashley wouldn't want it any other way."

"I'll help as much as I can too," put in Ellen.

"Thank-you; that's all for now but I will keep you informed. I'll be going to the hospital in the morning and will probably spend most of the day there. We'll know more when Ashley wakes up and I want to be there when she does if possible.

Denley went home that evening but only briefly. He needed the privacy of his home to allow himself the time to agonize over what had happened to Ashley. At the hospital he had to be calm and contain his emotions but at home he could let his feelings go. He wanted to be the one to sit by her bedside and hold her hand and soothe her. He wanted to be able to take her pain away and be the one to comfort her but he had to stand by and allow Elizabeth that position.

When Elizabeth arrived at the hospital the next morning Ashley still hadn't woke up. She was starting to run a fever and Dr. Denley was concerned about the infection. Elizabeth sat holding her hand for hours. Ashley didn't move or give any indication of returning to consciousness.

The nurse came and chased Elizabeth away so she could check the dressing over her stab wound and when she was finished Elizabeth returned to her side but there was still no sign of movement. She couldn't bear seeing Ashley look so battered. It hurt Elizabeth to see her like that. Her head was swathed in bandages and she had a few smaller ones on her face and arms along with some scratches and bruises. She looked so small and pale. She had to hang on for Katie's sake and she still wasn't out of danger.

"You should go get something to eat. I want to try to wake her up but I'll wait till you return. Go on, Ashley isn't going to wake up on her own."

Elizabeth dashed to a tea house close by and ordered a sandwich and some tea. She ate the sandwich quickly and didn't remember even tasting it. The tea was too weak but she finished it and dashed back to the hospital.

Dr Denley had Elizabeth stand back out of the way a bit while he tried talking softly to Ashley to rouse her. He tried gently nudging her but it didn't work. He finally used smelling salts and her eyelids began to flutter. "Ashley, do you know who I am and where you are? Do you know what happened to you?"

Ashley barely opened her eyes and then they closed again. Dr. Denley tried asking her again, "Do you remember what happened; do you know where you are?"

Her eyes fluttered again and she felt like her head was in a fog. She was confused and in pain. She couldn't seem to form words. The nurse tried to give her a bit of water and she slid back into deep black unconsciousness.

"I'll try again later even if all we accomplish is getting some water into her. With the fever she'll dehydrate and we need to get the fluids into her. The rest will hopefully come back in time. She's been through an awful ordeal. It might be good if she doesn't remember the attack but let's just take this one step at a time."

Elizabeth held her hand again, but now she talked softly to her. She talked about Katie, and how Maggie promised to take care of her. There was no response; not even a squeeze of her hand. Nothing to indicate she was hearing anything.

Dr. Denley was standing beside her, "You should go home and get some rest. We'll try again tomorrow."

Elizabeth took Dr. Denley's advice. Playing herself out would be of no benefit to Ashley and he had no idea how long it would take before she started to respond.

She was met at the door by a very anxious Maggie wanting to know every detail and was distressed when Elizabeth related how their attempts to wake her up went.

The next two days went much like the first. The nurses were checking bandages, sponging her forehead down with cool cloths trying to keep the fever down, treating infection and attempting to get some fluids into her.

Dr. Denley would sit by Ashley after Elizabeth went home in the evenings. He would check her pulse and check for reflexes. He would talk to her about anything he could think of.

On the fourth day there were some good improvements. Ashley's fever had started to go down. When Elizabeth arrived at the hospital Ashley was blinking her eyes trying to focus. Dr. Denley was changing her bandage on her side and she made a moaning sound like she was in pain. "I know it hurts Ashley but I have to keep the bandages clean. I'm almost done."

Elizabeth couldn't help but stare at the terrible cut in her side when the bandage was off. It looked like a jagged cut that was going to leave a horrible scar. With all the stitches to hold it together it looked even worse.

Do you know who I am? Ashley, do you know who I am?"

In a very low voice barely audible she answered, "The library."

"No Ashley, I'm Dr. Denley. Do you know where you are?"

Again in the same voice she said "library."

"That's where you were when something terrible happened. Now you're in the hospital. Do you remember what happened?"

"There's Blood everywhere. My side hurts, my head hurts."

"I know you're hurting. Let's concentrate on getting you better."

"Katie. Where's Katie?" Frantically she tried to get up but stabbing pains in her head and side made her cry out. She tried again but Dr. Denley was now holding her down. Her body was rigid.

"You have to lie still. Katie's ok love; Maggie's looking after Katie."

On hearing that she relaxed, closed her eyes and was out again.

Elizabeth just stood frozen on the spot watching what was happening. Hoping; praying that Ashley was going to be alright. She was remembering Katie's name and that was a start, other things were mixed up but hopefully that would clear up.

Margaret Golde was on today and she was asked to change the other dressings on Ashley's head and arms. While she did that Dr. Denley went over to talk to Elizabeth. "There is bound to be some confusion but that's a step in the right direction. It may take some time for her to get things straightened out in her mind."

The next few nights were troubled with memories being recalled to mind and she kept crying out William's name, along with other cries that only she would understand if she were conscious.

By the end of two weeks Ashley was able to recall some things that had happened. She did remember two boys running but couldn't remember why. She also remembered she was supposed to meet Elizabeth for tea but everything else after that was a blur. She was suffering terrible head aches but after she had been in the hospital two and a half weeks her head aches came a little less often. While they didn't come every day they were every bit as painful. When Dr. Denley finally allowed her to sit propped up on pillows the first time she let out a cry of pain. But gradually the pain eased up and Elizabeth was delighted to enter the hospital to see Ashley sitting slightly upright. She wanted to be home so badly that Dr. Denley decided to allow it. Her stitches had been removed and he knew she would be able to sit up unaided. He made Elizabeth promise that she would be getting plenty of bed rest and she was not allowed to tire herself out with Katie or be on the stairs. He also wanted to accompany her on the ride and make sure she was settled into her room. He would check on her four or five times a week and if they had any concerns they were to be sure to talk to him.

Maggie and Ellen had decided it would be best to have a room set up on the main floor so with the help of the cook's husband who tended to the yard and stables they moved furniture down so that she would be in familiar surroundings as much as possible.

After getting Ashley settled she began to complain of a head ache returning from the bumpy ride in the carriage so Dr. Denley stayed longer to make sure it eased up. Evening was creeping up so he was invited to remain for supper and thoroughly enjoyed not only the food but also the company. Since Sarah had left, he spent longer hours at the hospital and the remainder of his days and weekends were spent alone with his thoughts.

5
Road to Recovery

Denley's thoughts weren't of Sarah though. He found himself thinking of Ashley more often than just at work. While she had been under his care at the hospital he arrived earlier and stayed later. He found himself thinking about her even when he was tending to other patients and he would sit with her for long hours working with her to get her co-ordination back. He listened to her talk, and her speech was a little slower but he felt she would have a close to complete recovery. Now he would only see her at her home but he would make her call the last of the day. He wouldn't have an excuse to rush off.

Elizabeth began to notice the way he would look at Ashley and the way he would hold her hand to calm her down when she got frustrated. The kindness in his voice was becoming a little less professional and little more like a friend. Even little Katie was not making shy around him. Ellen began to set an extra plate on the table when he was there and so began a warm friendship with the whole household. He hated leaving for his small home at the end of the evening.

Ashley would thrash around and break into a sweat during the nights and woke Maggie up often. She was beginning to have nightmares about what happened and was finally able to talk to the police about it. She confirmed two boys had attacked her but was unable to give them a description. They really didn't have much to go on but for some reason they didn't believe it was a random attack.

Elizabeth had helped her try to remember other things and helped fill in some of the blanks that Ashley had trouble with but she could only help with information that Ashley had revealed to her and it frustrated Ashley when she tried to remember other things. There were bits and pieces of her life that just seemed like a closed book to her. Other things came to her clearly. She was going to have to stay here not only because she needed help tending to Katie but Elizabeth, Maggie and Ellen were like family now.

As Ashley continued to recover Dr. Denley came by less frequent. He didn't want to wear out his welcome. Her stab wound had left a pink scar on her side that was a bitter reminder of what had happened. Dr. Denley told her the visibility would lessen in time but would probably not totally disappear. She seemed to be getting headaches less often but when she did get one it was usually a bad one and more often than not it was when she was in an upright position. It was going to be something she may have to cope with for some time while the healing continued.

Ashley's close call with death made her realize she needed to have something in writing so Katie's needs would be looked after. Thinking long and hard on it she decided to ask Elizabeth if she would look after Katie if anything happened. Elizabeth's eyes filled with tears to be considered in that way. "I don't want Katie torn away from everyone she knows and everything she is familiar with. So if you are willing, I would like to have a legal written agreement done up stating my wishes. You will of course need to know that Katie's last name is Radcliff, not Grey. Grey is my maiden name and I have been using it to prevent William's parents from finding me. I want her to eventually get to know them but if something should happen to me you will be able to prepare her for it when the time is right.

"So when you say Radcliff and you came from Newcastle you are referring to the Radcliff's of the shipyard?"

"That would be correct. Please don't get me wrong. I want her grandparents to get to know her but I have to find her uncle first. I don't want Mrs. Radcliff to control Katie's life expecting her to take her sons place."

It was Ashley's first outing since the attack and Elizabeth had gone with her to the solicitor to have the papers done up. It was the same solicitor Elizabeth had seen that day on the important matter she needed to tend to. She had Clive removed as sole beneficiary and unknown to Ashley she had it changed to include her and Katie, along with Ellen and Maggie. It was also with the provision that all staff still employed at the Thatcher residence would be cared for financially.

A couple of days after his last house call on Ashley, Sarah showed up and wanted to see Dr. Denley. They met at a small tea house and he was curious what brought her back.

"I had thought you might come after me, or try to stop me from going. I was upset when I wrote the letter I left you. I want you back in my life. I still love you and want to marry you. Let's just run off and come back husband and wife. We could live in London and you would be able to set up a practice there." She reached out to grab his hand in an attempt to get an affirming squeeze of the hand only to have him brush her off. A quick little pout appeared on her mouth that made her so attractive and at that moment he was surprised that he didn't need to check his emotions. He actually felt nothing for her now and this obviously made her attempts futile.

'No I don't think so. I think what you wrote in that letter was exactly how you feel. You said you knew it wouldn't work out."

"No, I was upset when I wrote that. I didn't mean it; any of it. You have to believe me." She pleaded.

"Actually I believe you meant every word of it. I started looking back and all the signs were there. I know it wouldn't work out now either and I think you saved us a lot of heart ache. I want to leave it at that." With those words spoken he rose to his feet wished her good day and walked away without looking back. Walking out of the diner he came face to face with Elizabeth and Ashley.

This was awkward. He didn't want to be rude and walk away but he also knew that Sarah would be coming out right behind him. And he was right. She was calling after him. "Denley we need to talk still, I'm not finished; I'm sorry."

Right in front of Ashley and Elizabeth he turned to Sarah and in response told her not to make it more difficult than it already was. "Go back to your family in London Sarah. We both know that you wouldn't be happy here." She glared at him and realized they weren't alone so she turned on her heels and walked off in a huff.

"I'm sorry you witnessed that. It was just bad timing." Feeling a need to explain he continued, "Sarah broke off our engagement some time before the explosion at the mine but was having second thoughts. I came to realize that it would have been a mistake to marry her. We are from two different worlds. She just wasn't prepared for me to let her go so easily."

Elizabeth started putting some pieces together remembering how he looked at Ashley on his visits especially when he didn't think anyone was watching. He was falling in love with Ashley and she had no clue. She was just his patient and as far as she had known, he was engaged. "I'm sorry to hear about that. Would you like to join us for a cup of tea? Just pretend we didn't catch that conversation and we'll do the same."

"Don't be sorry. It was actually for the best. It only took me a couple of weeks to realize it but I wasn't expecting her to show up again. I could use a cup of tea though." So turning around they all walked back into the diner that Dr. Denley and Sarah had just walked out of. "Just one more thing; could you please drop the doctor title. Just call me Denley, I'll explain while we have the tea."

Ashley was the first to bring the subject up again after the waitress left their table. "So you want us to call you by your last name?"

"Denley is my first name. When I was studying to be a doctor there was another student that had the same last name. We just decided to make it easier by going by our first names and for me it just stuck."

"Well then when we see you professionally we'll use doctor and when we see you as a friend we'll drop it." They enjoyed their tea and the conversation that went with it. After that they parted company but not before Elizabeth invited him to come by for a meal again.

Ashley was played out by the time they arrived home and only spent a few minutes with Katie before she had to lie down for a rest. It had been quite a day of revelations.

Denley went home early that same day. His stomach was twisted in a knot. What must Ashley think of him dismissing Sarah, telling her to go back to her family in front of her like that? She acted like everything was okay but was it just a pretense? All he could think about was how Ashley looked; her hair sweeping to one side to cover where her hair had to be clipped short to stitch up the cuts. Her pale skin and big brown eyes that held a sadness that made him just want to gather her up in his arms to protect and care for her. He didn't even know if that would ever be possible. Well he would never know unless he tried. He would wait a couple of days and then drop by to accept the invite he had received and maybe invite her out for a carriage ride. The leaves on the trees were starting to change and a ride through the park would be nice as long as the weather held. If not he would just have to be creative and think of something else. He felt better after making that decision.

Denley arrived early on a Saturday afternoon with the hopes of the invitation for dinner to be repeated and was happily surprised when Elizabeth did just that. "I thought Katie might enjoy a carriage ride through the park with Ashley of course."

Quickly Maggie readied Katie for the ride and Ashley went for a sweater just in case it got a bit cool. Denley took Ashley's hand and helped her up onto the seat and handed Katie to her and then walking around the front of the horse he gave it a pat on its soft muzzle and then climbed up beside Ashley. He tucked a blanket around her legs and gave the reigns a flick putting the horse into motion.

It was a beautiful day for a ride through the park, the colors of the leaves were turning gold, orange and red and the air was not too cool. Katie started to act up so he pulled on the reigns and the carriage came to a halt. He could see Ashley was tiring a bit trying to hold her still so he reached over and took Katie from her arms and held her in his arms. Katie settled right down. "It seems that all she wanted was for you to hold her. I guess she misses you coming around."

Denley gave a bit of a happy laugh. "It seems she's got her way." With that he settled Katie on his knee and adjusted his grip on the reigns to control the horse. He gave the reigns another flick and they were on the move again. Elizabeth was sitting on the front porch when they arrived back and so she went over and took Katie from Denley's arms so he could climb down and help Ashley. By the time he got around to her side she had the blanket neatly folded and placed where he had been sitting and was ready to be helped down. He knew Ashley was played out from the outing so taking Ashley by the waist to steady her she almost floated to the ground. She allowed him to take her by the arm and lead her inside to a comfortable chair.

"It seems our Katie has missed Denley. She was fussing and calmed right down when he took her from me."

"Well that doesn't surprise me. She had really taken to him when he was coming by almost daily to check on you. Perhaps Denley, you shouldn't be such a stranger." Denley had wished those last words had come from Ashley but at least he had the opening needed to come by from time to time and Ashley didn't object.

Maggie popped her head out the door to announce dinner was almost ready. Ashley excused herself so she could freshen up and the rest followed suit. They enjoyed a delicious meal and conversation before they retired to the sitting room for an after dinner drink.

Elizabeth spilled her drink and apologized for her clumsiness as she slipped from the room. Ashley entertained Denley for a good 15 minutes before she returned. Denley didn't want the evening to end but he didn't want Ashley to get played out so he stood as Elizabeth entered and thanked her for a wonderful evening. Then turning to Ashley he thanked her for accompanying him on the ride through the park.

Over the next few weeks Denley started coming by for short visits and offered carriage rides through the park until the air became too cold for it. Through the winter months they would sit and play games with the fire crackling in the background.

Elizabeth could see there was a definite attraction growing at least on the part of Denley but wasn't too sure if it was returned. She could see how kind, and patient he was not only with Ashley but also with Katie. Besides being widowed and everything else that has happened to her in the past year she was going to need some time. Perhaps she still looked at Denley as her doctor and didn't see the attraction changing.

They started to expect Denley to show up every Wednesday and Saturday. He always made sure he had time for Katie before her naps or bedtime. December was an especially hard month being the anniversary of William's death. It became very obvious one evening when Denley was playing with Katie and Ashley was sitting watching. Her eyes filled with tears as she thought of how it should have been William down there with her. But of coarse she would never have met Elizabeth, Maggie and Denley if he was still alive. She remembered how excited they were when they found out she was pregnant. William couldn't wait to introduce Ashley to his parents and she was looking forward to it too. He had promised they would buy a house and settle in Newcastle and make it their home. Instead she was sitting here watching Denley play with her daughter.

Denley looked up and noticed Ashley seemed to be lost in thought and then looking closer he noticed the tears. Elizabeth noticed what was happening and scooped Katie up to get her ready for bed. Now alone in the room with Ashley he went over and sat down beside her. He gently tilted her head up and dabbed her cheeks with a handkerchief and then the tears came in a flood. "William was killed around this time last year."

He put his arms around her and allowed her to huddle into his chest and cry until she was drained. Then feeling embarrassed she pulled herself together, "I'm sorry. I cried for William a year ago, I thought I was past this.

"You've been through more this year than most. It's understandable." With his arm tucked around her they just sat side by side in a comfortable silence until it was time for Denley to leave. Ashley walked to the door with him and when she opened the door she noticed snow flakes were just starting to fall again.

"I better get myself home while I can still get the carriage to move."

He climbed into his carriage and gave the reigns a snap.

Through the winter the days got shorter and colder. When it was too cold to be outside they sat by the fire and listened to it crackle. Ashley and Elizabeth sat and did their needle point, Elizabeth taught Ashley how to work the spools to make lace, and they did some sewing for the coming spring. Some days were nice enough to go out and let Katie play in the snow and Denley would take them skating on a pond that had been cleared off. Other days the snow came down so hard they didn't think it was ever going to stop. Denley wasn't able to come as often through the winter as it was harder to get around in the ice and snow. December rolled into January and then into February and March and with that the days started to lengthen again and the snow conditions began to ease up.

It took Ashley by surprise when Denley showed up one Tuesday afternoon and asked if she could accompany him on a medical emergency. "A small boy-Robby has fallen down a bank and his family is still trying to get him up to safety. They want me to be there as quickly as possible. I could really use an assistant. It's on the other side of town though. I hope that won't trouble you."

"The only trouble it will be is if you keep standing there talking." Hastily pulling on her coat and boots she wrapped a scarf around her neck, grabbed a pair of gloves and asking Maggie to watch Katie they hurried out the door.

It wasn't hard to find the area with the number of people gathered and they only had about a 15 minute wait before the little boy was pulled back up. He looked to be about seven years old. Quickly Denley began checking for any major injuries. He was cold but conscious. He had a broken leg that would need to be set but he also had some bruising to the stomach and some pain there. Ashley held the boy still while Denley put the splint on his leg and holding him steady while he assessed him for any more major injuries. Through it all Ashley kept talking to him trying to keep him calm. She had a soothing voice that seemed to help. As she talked to him Denley checked him over more closely concentrating on his abdomen. Denley was concerned of internal bleeding and wanted him taken to the hospital as quickly as possible.

Ashley was consoling the parents while they got the boy onto a cart. Denley went with the boy and the parents went with Ashley in Denley's carriage. At the hospital he was rushed into an examining room and the nurses left Ashley sitting with the parents. She sat holding the mothers hand in an effort to console her. When Denley finally appeared he told the parents they could sit with him. "I want him to stay for the night so we can keep an eye on him. He has a few stitches and his leg has been set. We are trying to get his body temperature up a bit but he should be fine. Both parents thanked him and a nurse took them to his bedside.

"You must be cold and exhausted. I can offer you a quiet room and a cup of tea to help warm you but I can't leave for about an hour now. I want to keep a watch on Robby for a bit. Are you okay with that?"

"That sounds just fine."

He led her to a small office and offered her a seat and then disappeared for a couple of minutes. He returned with two cups of tea and sat facing her. Handing her a cup of tea he smiled at her and thanked her for the help. "You have a nice touch with people and they seem to respond to you nicely. When we can get away from here will you join me for dinner?"

"I would like to but I need to tend to Katie. I don't like to just presume upon Maggie." Watching his smile fade a bit she came back quickly, "Unless you don't mind eating a bit later. I'm free for the evening once she's sleeping." His smile broadened and he sat back and drank his tea.

When he knew for sure the boy would be fine they left the hospital and headed for what Ashley now called home. Katie was all smiles when they walked in and she started squirming so Elizabeth set her down. She started to totter then fell back on her butt, crawled the rest of the way past Ashley to Denley and tried to stand, pulling herself up by his pant leg. "Well it looks like Katie is getting around pretty good."

"She'll be running to you when you walk in the door before you know it." He picked her up and gave her a twirl in the air before handing her over to Ashley.

Denley sat with Elizabeth and told her how the afternoon went while Ashley tended to Katie and settled her down for the night. She also decided to freshen up a bit and change her dress to something a little fancier. She came down wearing a floor length gown that was a mix of gold and rust colors.

As she entered the room Denley stood and cleared his throat. "I feel a little under dressed now. You look lovely."

"Thank-you," she smiled and turned to Elizabeth, "I've asked Maggie to listen for Katie but she'll probably be good for the night. I'll just get my coat."

They walked to the door and Denley helped Ashley into her coat, she pulled on a pair of gloves and adjusted a hat that matched nicely. Elizabeth watched from the window as he helped Ashley up into the carriage and he had a bit of spring in his step as he strode around to get in beside her. "Well Maggie, what do you think? Don't they look good together?"

"I didn't notice before, I mean I guess I wasn't paying that much attention. But now you mention it-yes, yes they do. Do you think they'll get married?"

"I believe it could be a very good possibility, at least that's probably the direction Denley is hoping for."

With Denley's hand guiding Ashley by her elbow they followed the head waitress to a secluded little table. Denley noticed a few heads turning and it made him realize how beautiful Ashley was, not that he needed reminded. Last fall he never would have believed he would be sitting here with her. He didn't even know if she was going to recover from her injuries. He took the liberty of ordering for her and they enjoyed a pleasant meal and conversation. Laying his napkin down on his plate he looked at her and took a deep breath, "This has been an eventful day. I want to thank-you for coming with me. I think I have already said that, but you have a really nice way with people especially with children. You don't intimidate people; they can see that you're sincere." Well that wasn't what he wanted to say. But how could he say what was on his mind? How could he tell her the affect her presence has on his heart?

After a pleasant evening and being seen to the door they wished each other a good night and for Denley, his ride home in the carriage was a time for his thoughts. He wasn't sure if Ashley had feelings for him in any other form except as a close friend and he was having a hard time summing up the courage to let his feelings be known to her verbally. What probably was holding him back was the fear of loosing what he already had. He didn't remember any of these feelings when he had become engaged to Sarah.

As for Ashley, when she entered the house everything was in turmoil. Elizabeth was in a dreadful state. Ellen and Maggie were busy packing her traveling trunk and carpet bag. A telegram had come to inform Elizabeth that her sister Martha desperately needed her presence. Clive had been found dead and the situation was a mess. Elizabeth would be taking the earliest coach out in the morning to be by her sister's side and stay until after the funeral or longer if Martha needed her.

"Usually when I go to my sister's I give Ellen the time off to visit her relatives. If Maggie stays on with you Ashley will that be sufficient? Everything else will remain the same."

"Oh that will be fine. Does Maggie not want the time off?"

"No she has no family. She considers us her family and she wants to stay on with you and help with Katie. I really don't know how long I will be gone for. If it looks like I'll be gone for too long I'll send a telegram to let you know."

That was a relief to Ashley as she still played out at times trying to tend to Katie's needs. She was becoming quite a handful and Ashley had been relying quite heavily on Maggie's help.

Elizabeth's trunk and carpet bag sat ready at the door to be carried out in the early morning hours.

6
The Purse

The trip to Birmingham seemed longer than usual but Elizabeth was anxious to be by Martha's side. The telegram was very short with no details. Elizabeth could not believe Clive was dead. How, why, what happened? Poor Martha, Clive was her whole life. How was she going to cope with his loss? The loss of her husband almost put her in the grave and now she would have to put Clive in the grave. What would that do to Martha?

Elizabeth was picked up by one of her staff; not one she had met before. She was taken to Martha's but Martha was being kept sedated and so Elizabeth would have to wait until tomorrow to talk to her. Her room was prepared for her just the way she liked it and after freshening up bit a tray was brought up for her with tea and crumpets.

The next morning Elizabeth was up early and decided it best to dress in black. Although she had been mad at Clive for trying to set Ashley up as a thief she would never have wanted anything bad to happen to him. She made her way to Martha's room and tapped lightly on the door before entering. Martha was lying in her bed awake but looking very frail and still slightly limber from the effects of the sedation. Elizabeth walked over and gave her a hug and a kiss on the cheek before adjusting the pillows to prop her up. Then sitting down facing her and not saying a word looked at her sister, waiting until she was ready to tell her what happened.

"Apparently my son had accumulated a large amount of debt within a gambling ring and was murdered. At least that's what the police have come up with so far." Starting to sob, she continued on, "That's only part of it though. It does get worse. I don't know how to even begin to tell you the rest." Reaching into her night stand she pulled out a purse that looked a little familiar to Elizabeth. Martha handed it to her and began to sob again and held her handkerchief tightly in her fingers. "You'll understand when you open it. I found it within Clive's belongings and thought it might belong to a lady friend of his but…"

Elizabeth opened it and looked at the contents and paled in total disbelief and horror. It was Ashley's belongings she was staring at. The only way he could have this purse was if he had something to do with the attack on her. She couldn't believe that Clive had been the reason for that terrible attack and Ashley had paid dearly. The head aches that still came from time to time and her talking was still a little slower. If you hadn't known Ashley before the attack you probably wouldn't notice but for those who knew her it is still slightly noticeable, and her energy was a little less than normal.

Clive had to have stayed in town after being told to leave that day. He may have been watching for the opportunity and may have even watched Elizabeth go into the solicitor's office and if that was the case he would have known she was having him removed from her will. He would have been out for revenge and Ashley was the innocent victim of his planned assault. How could her nephew have been capable of such evil?

"It belongs to the young lady that was attacked; the one that lives with you doesn't it? I was hoping I was wrong, but I'm not am I?"

Elizabeth wasn't sure if she should tell Martha what had happened just before the attack or if it was better to say nothing about it and in the end decided to say nothing. She decided Clive had already put Martha through enough with out adding more to his list of evils. "I'm sorry Martha. I wish I could tell you it belonged to someone else too."

Elizabeth stayed on for a month to make sure Martha would be ok. "If you get too lonely in this old house you can always pack up and move in with me. I still have lots of empty rooms."

"No, all my memories with my husband and Clive are all here and I have the different socials and bridge parties I attend. I'll be fine, really I will."

Elizabeth was getting anxious to be home before the hot weather came. Traveling by coach in the heat is terribly uncomfortable. Though she wasn't looking forward to the conversation she would be having with Ashley. She couldn't bear the fact that one of her family members had caused Ashley so much grief.

Denley offered to meet Elizabeth at the station. It was Monday but it gave him an excuse to go by her place. He took every opportunity he could find just to see Ashley and Katie. Elizabeth looked tired from her journey and Denley noticed she wasn't herself. "I trust your journey was ok."

"Yes, fine thank-you. I'm sorry if I am a bit off. I've news to tell Ashley that I'm not particularly looking forward to. Perhaps I can persuade you to stay to dinner. Your presence may help keep her calm." With that Elizabeth confided in Denley the whole story feeling a huge weight being unloaded off her shoulders.

"Dr. Denley at your service," he teased as they neared the gates at the entrance. Pulling the horse to a halt at the doors he helped Elizabeth down and opened the door for her. Mr.

Whitfield was always ready for anyone arriving so he could lead their horse to the stables until they were ready to leave. Sometimes Elizabeth didn't know how he knew to be at the front entrance but that was part of his job and he was good at it. He probably heard the horse's hooves hitting the ground and from where the cottage that he and his wife lived in was situated he could look out the window and see them coming.

There was a squeal of excitement from Katie and she made her way as quickly as she could to Elizabeth's waiting arms. "Oh how I have missed you Katie." With a kiss on the cheek she was squirming out of her arms and into Denley's.

Everyone watching started to laugh at her antics. Elizabeth handed her a parcel all wrapped up and they enjoyed watching as Ashley helped Katie into the package to reveal a cloth doll.

"Ellen, when did you arrive back?"

"I returned two days ago. My sister and her husband had planned a trip away and they couldn't change their plans. It was a long enough visit though."

"Well it's nice to have you back. There are more packages in my luggage if you don't mind putting them out for me, and I would like to have a few words with Ashley in the study and Denley will join us."

Ashley looked a little puzzled but made her way to the study with Denley closing the door behind them.

"I've confided in Denley what I have to tell you Ashley so I hope you don't mind him being in here. This is more difficult than I thought it was going to be but I have found out the person responsible for the attack you suffered. There is no easy way to tell you so I'll just come out with it; it was Clive. After his death Martha found your purse in with his belongings. I am so sorry for all that you suffered at the hands of my nephew. I can't begin to make up for it." With Elizabeth's voice full of emotion she pulled

Ashley's small purse out of a bag she was holding and handed it to Ashley.

Elizabeth and Denley watched Ashley as the news sank in and she sat looking at her purse. "I don't understand. It was two boys; I remember two boys attacked me." Then it clicked, "You mean Clive had those two boys attack me. Did he pay them? I can't imagine why he hated me so. I know I didn't care for him but to hate me so much—why?"

"I can only imagine he felt his inheritance was being threatened by your presence. He, being my only relative next to Martha stood to inherit a great deal. He had accumulated a large gambling debt and was probably hoping to get help from me and lost that opportunity with the last stunt he tried to pull off when he was here. He knew everything had changed after I sent him away when he tried to make it look like you were stealing from me. That day we went to town he probably watched me drop you off at the library and what I never told you, was that I went into the solicitor's office to remove his name from my will because I was so mad at him."

Ashley began to pale and her stomach began to churn. Denley could see she was visibly shaken and took her hands in his to steady them. Ashley then looked up at Elizabeth and realized the anguish she must be feeling. "Elizabeth, this isn't your fault. You couldn't possibly think you are responsible for what happened. It's something you had no control over." She pulled her hands free and turned to Elizabeth and gave her a hug. "You've been agonizing over this the whole time you were away haven't you? Please don't feel that way. I would like it if you informed your sister Martha that I don't hold it against her either. Clive was a grown man responsible for his own actions."

Denley walked over to a small counter and poured three drinks and handed them out. "I think a good drink before dinner would be just what the doctor orders to steady the nerves."

They all gave a bit of a chuckle and finished their drinks before heading to the dinning room for dinner. Katie made it quite obvious that she wanted to be sitting between Denley and Elizabeth so Ashley let her have her way when Elizabeth offered to feed her and Denley said he had no problem wearing a bit of potato.

Ashley waited until she was in the privacy of her room that evening to open the purse and look at the contents. She really hadn't remembered what was in it after so much time had passed. She noticed the paper with the name Rosie Boyle on it and sat staring at the name. It sounded familiar but why? Was it someone she met? The rest of the items in the purse were just things one would carry. She would dispose of the purse. She didn't think she would want to keep it now but her eyes fell on the piece of paper again and she knew she was going to puzzle over that name until she figured it out.

Her sleep was not a restful one that night. She tossed and turned and then when sleep finally claimed her tired body the visions came in sweeps. The Library came into her visions so real she could almost smell the books. The name Rosie Boyle came to her from a news paper and then Williams name flashed in her memory. The attack outside the Library happened to her and it was like living it all over again. Was Clive somewhere in the distance watching with some kind of sick pleasure as the two boys rushed in on her pushing her down violently and thrusting the knife into her side? Did it give him some satisfaction to see her suffer in pain? She let out a few agonizing cries and then someone seemed to soothe her back to sleep. It was Dr. Denley's voice telling her to be calm, that she was going to be ok.

Then her mind flashed back farther. To the day William and she had arrived at his parent's home. It was huge and terribly cold and there seemed to be little affection shared in this family. Even the introduction to his parents was very unemotional; one would call it cold and perfunctory. His mother Pauline had taken to her sleeping chambers and rarely came out. William left Ashley sitting on the couch with his mother and rang for tea to be brought up before following his father Willard into the study where a yelling match ensued. Ashley could hear the not so quiet words spoken between the two. She couldn't make out all of the conversation but the first part was about his fathers thoughts of whom he had chosen as a wife. As accomplished as Ashley is it was still beneath the wealth that the Radcliff's possessed. Willard was the owner of a very large shipyard and owned large portions of property both in Newcastle and surrounding areas. William was trying to talk his father into searching for Denny his brother and bringing him back if nothing else for the sake of his mother who was pining for her beloved son. His father then began screaming that Denny was a huge let down and a disgrace to the family name. "Never will he set foot into this house in my presence again," his father shouted and stormed out of the room slamming the door behind.

Then Ashley's breathing came in gulps as she relived the news of William's death. William had left on a false pretense of business but he was searching for his brother and Ashley was going to try and coax his mother out of her room. The news shattered his mother so deeply that she refused to be comforted for weeks and then she became intensely interested in Ashley and the baby she was carrying. For a bit it was fine but then she became obsessive. She started watching Ashley's every move in the house and even when Ashley walked through the grounds. Everywhere Ashley went his mother was always watching. She began to talk about nurses and nannies and even hiring a wet nurse. She talked about the best schools and which ones they should look into. It was as if she was planning for this baby to replace her son's and Ashley could slowly feel her control slipping away. His father Willard was so cold to Ashley she could hardly believe William; her caring, loving and totally devoted husband could be related in any manner to this man.

It wasn't until Pauline twisted her ankle and was instructed by the doctor to keep off it for a couple of days that the opportunity became available for Ashley to get away. She didn't hesitate for fear the moment would slip away. She knew where she had to go. She had to go to the last known destination of William. She had to find William's brother and somehow reunite him with his mother even if it had to be kept secret from William's father. Pauline needed to have a relationship with her grandchild and the only way that could happen was to find William's brother and so when Ashley left it was with no malice intended.

Ashley was still breathing in gulps when Maggie began to talk to her calmly. Ashley blinked a few times and realized she had been having a nightmare and gradually her breathing calmed down and Maggie returned to her room. Ashley laid there afraid to close her eyes again but eventually she could ward it off no longer and a restless sleep claimed her again.

Maggie slipped into Katie's room and took her down for breakfast in the morning. Elizabeth was already up as well and questioned Maggie about the noise she heard during the night. Maggie enlightened her as much as she could and it was decided they would allow Ashley the room she needed to work through her feelings and try to keep Katie occupied as much as possible.

When Ashley finally appeared she looked pale and tired. There was no need for words. Elizabeth took her by the hand and gave it a reassuring squeeze. Ashley spent the day digesting everything that had been revealed yesterday and the memories that were restored during the night. Well at least the name Rosie Boyle wasn't such a mystery. Perhaps finding this person would be the challenge now. She wasn't sure how she got through the day but was relieved when the end of it finally arrived. She collapsed into bed and slept like she hadn't slept in a long time.

By noon of the following day Ashley was back to herself again and decided on a trip into town. Elizabeth was tired and decided to stay and keep Katie, with Maggie's help. Dressed in a milk chocolate silk and lace dress that almost dusted the floor as she walked, she added gloves and a straw boater hat that complemented her face nicely and giving Katie a hug and a kiss on the cheek she was out the door.

She wasn't sure how to go about finding Rosie Boyle and decided on a quick stop at the clinic. Denley may know her or how to go about finding her. He was just leaving the clinic as she was getting out of the carriage and he came to assist her. "To what do I owe this pleasant surprise? You're not ill are you?" Not letting her answer he continued, "No of coarse your not. You look too lovely to be ill."

"Well, thank-you," she blushed. "I actually came to ask you if you know a woman by the name of Rosie Boyle or how I would go about finding her."

He raised an eyebrow in amusement. "I'm just on my way out for lunch. Please join me, and after lunch I can introduce you personally. I am curious why you are asking of her but then you haven't lived here long enough to hear of her perhaps."

Sitting out on a small patio she sipped her tea and while he ate she explained the piece of paper with the name on it and the terrible night she had when she recalled everything. "I feel like my life just spun out of control and now I'm trying to get everything back together."

As it turned out Rosie Boyle is known to a large number of people in the area, as she runs a boarding house in the east end of town not quite in the slums. She is a pleasant heavy woman too short for her size but with a bubbly personality. Ashley guessed her to be in her mid 50's. Her face lit up when she realized it was Denley that walked in her door. "Aye, this must be your lady friend. I heard you were gettin married. You brung her by for me to git a look at her did ya?"

"No, this is a friend though. I'm not getting married Rosie. It didn't work out, but I did come to introduce this young lady to you." After the introduction he decided to give Ashley her space and told her he would wait in the carriage for her.

"Well love what can I do ya for?"

Ashley explained her reason for coming. "I just wanted to know when you found William if he said anything that would be helpful. Was he conscious?"

"Oh, aye he was conscious all right, but not for long love. He said, 'Doctor Denley,' took a few breaths and said your name, an that was it, he never woke up. He must have bin asking for a Doctor but Denley was in London round bout that time and it wouldn't have changed things. He was bad off. I'm sorry for your loss and I'm sorry I've not been much help.'

"Thank you for your time, I'll not keep you any longer, and Denley is on his lunch break. I shouldn't keep him waiting out there too long."

I'll see you out the door; I'll not let Denley go without sayin goodbye. You know he comes by ever so often. When I get someone in here bad off, I mean; and I have to send for a doctor"

"Well thank-you again."

"Aye a real gentleman, he is," Rosie acknowledged with a wide smile of approval as he helped Ashley into the carriage. "You'll not be a stranger now."

Denley gave the reigns a snap and the horse gave a snort before moving into action. "Did you find what you were looking for?"

"No, but interestingly he asked for you by name just before he died. Well, he was asking for you as Dr. Denley. Rosie said it would have done no good, he wouldn't have survived; and you were in London at the time."

"That's probably around the time I met Sarah. I worked in the hospital in London for a time to learn a new procedure." He turned the horse down a street she hadn't been on before and said he wanted to check on someone before he headed back. "I hope you don't mind but I'm already here."

"I don't mind, is it something I can help with?"

"If you would like to, I need to change a bandage on a man that was injured at the mine last week. He almost lost his arm. It was caught between two carts and I worry still about infection and blood poisoning."

By the time they got back to town he didn't want to return to the clinic. He was enjoying the afternoon with Ashley and didn't want it to end so soon. He tacked a note on the door saying he would return tomorrow. "May I offer you a ride home or are there other matters you need to finish with?"

"I wanted to walk through the shops and see what they have for summer stock. I haven't had an opportunity to shop in so long. You're welcome to walk with me if you like."

They walked through the shops and talked amiably about almost anything. They were quite comfortable together. After making several purchases, Denley insisted on carrying her parcels for her. She started to lead the way out the door when a small child caught Ashley's attention. She was pulling a wagon that had some small puppies in it. Impulsively Ashley headed across the road to look at them. By the time Denley caught up she had already scooped up the runt of the litter and was talking to it as if it understood her every word.

Denley reach into his pocket and paid the little girl for the puppy and as Ashley was trying to protest all he said was, "Katie needs a puppy. But my hands are full so you'll have to carry that little parcel on your own. I don't think Elizabeth will mind. It seems to me she has spoken fondly of a dog she had a number of years ago."

Ashley smiled and thanked Denley. "I think now I'll have to go home. I can't carry this little thing around town. We'll have to think of a name for…" she stopped and looked under its back legs, "her. She looks like a little ball of white fluff. How about Fluffy or Snowball, they both fit her?"

"I like Snowball for a name and it has those little black round eyes that look like bits of coal," he said as they walked back towards the clinic where his horse was waiting. He put Ashley's parcels up into the back of the open carriage and placed the puppy into a box so he could help Ashley up into the seat then handed the puppy back to her to hold. He walked over to where Mr. Whitfield was waiting for Ashley and told him to just follow them back to her place.

He then went and took his seat next to Ashley and took up the reigns.

When they arrived back Denley handed Ashley's parcels over to Ellen and they were directed to the garden where Katie was entertaining Elizabeth in her whimsical way.

When she noticed them coming into view she immediately turned towards Denley until she spotted the puppy. Her eyes lit up and she made a sharp turn that caused her to stumble and land on her bottom. Ashley set the puppy down and it romped over to Katie. Ashley and Denley went over to show her how to handle a puppy gently.

"Katie's getting around very quickly now isn't she," Denley said as he scooped her up along with the puppy.

"Sometimes too fast; she can keep us running from one thing to the next. I'm sure she plays Maggie out as well at times."

Elizabeth motioned to them "Won't you join me for some Ice Tea? I'll have two more glasses brought out."

They sat at the table and Denley sat Katie down on a blanket close by so they could protect Snowball if she needed it and were amused at her attempts to say the puppy's name. He turned to Elizabeth then, "I hope you don't mind the puppy. I seem to remember you talking fondly of one you used to have otherwise I would never have presumed to bring one with out your permission."

That evening after Denley had left she sat up with Elizabeth and told her about everything she had remembered and about finding Rosie Boyle. Elizabeth was the only person Ashley had confided in with everything. "I feel like every time I go to town I am looking over my shoulder. I'm sure William's mother Pauline will come looking for me. She will want a connection with Katie, but the way she was before I left, she'll want control. They have money and I'm sure she will use it to her advantage. Now even the trail I thought I was following to find her other son seems to have grown cold."

"Perhaps it is not as bad as you think. Maybe it's as it should be and you need to get on with your own life. It seems to me there is a very fine gentleman that is hoping you will notice him as more than just a friend and he seems to adore Katie too."

"I've noticed Denley's attentions for a bit now and I do like him but…"

"If you have feelings for him don't wait too long or he might just slip away. Have you thought of confiding in him? You may want to be honest with him in whatever you decide to do. He is a decent man and deserves that much."

"You're right of course. I need to start thinking of Katie too. She absolutely loves Denley. He would be a good father; I know that. This coming Saturday I'll talk with him and by the time the evening is finished he'll at least know what has brought me here and how I feel. The rest will be up to him. I'll send word to him and see if he will come earlier Saturday. We can go to the park for a bit of a picnic and I can talk to him in private there. And now if you will excuse me I am so tired. It's been a long day and I would like to turn in."

"Yes of course. I am quite ready to turn in as well."

When Ashley finally retired to her room she saw the packages she had purchased on the bed. She had almost forgotten about them. Starting with the smallest package, she unwrapped it to reveal a dress for Katie. Now that she was walking it was time to buy her a fancy dress. It was a soft blue cotton but with a lace collar, little puff sleeves, and plenty of lace on the skirt. The next package was the dress for her. She held it up to herself and with her one hand holding the waist in place she twirled in front of a mirror. This dress was a rose color, different from most of the pinks she had seen. It buttoned down the front but came to a V at the waist, with folds of material that fell to the floor gracefully. There was no collar on it but instead it was a rounded neckline that allowed for a necklace to be shown off and sleeves that had an interesting tuck in them. Her wardrobe was coming together nicely after having to leave most of it behind when she left William's family. The last package was a hat box containing a hat that was to go with the dress and opening it to take a glimpse at it before readying herself for bed she noticed a small package gently placed inside the box off to the side of the hat. Unfolding the tissue carefully revealed a small pin with crystals matching the colors of her dress like they were made for each other. Denley must have picked it out when she was looking for the dress for Katie and busy talking to the sales clerk. Now looking at the hat she noticed that it matched the hat pin sticking in the hat. She hadn't received jewelry from a gentleman since she was courted by William and the sentiment was touching. When Saturday came it was going to be a little easier to tell him how she felt.

7
A Surprise Visitor

As Denley was dressing for work the next morning he whistled a tune as he wondered if Ashley had noticed the gift in the hat box. It wasn't expensive but it would give her an indication of how he felt; hopefully the feelings would be returned. About an hour after seeing patients the waiting room cleared and he sat at his desk to do a bit of reading. Looking up when the door opened a shocked expression passed over his face. There standing in the doorway was his mother Pauline Radcliff. They hadn't seen each other in two years and he immediately rushed to his feet to greet her with a warm embrace.

He was about to receive a couple of big blows though. Pauline sat across the desk from him and smiled, "Son you're a hard person to find but no wonder. You don't use your last name. Not to worry, now I've found you I'm not letting you out of my sight but I am sorry to say I have some bad news for you and I'm not sure where to begin. So from the start; your brother William married and brought his wife to meet us. She was a lovely girl, though your father didn't approve. Well William had to go on a business trip and left the young lady with us and my poor William never returned home." She dabbed her eyes and continued, "We received news that he had been beaten so badly he died from his injuries." When she saw the reaction of her words she quickly grabbed for his hands and made her way around the desk to hold him in her arms to comfort him. "I thought you might of known, perhaps being the doctor to attend to him but obviously I was wrong."

"Why would you think I knew? I haven't spoken to any family members since I set up practice here. Father made it clear I was not to destroy his precious name. That's why I go by my first name."

"I thought, well, because the telegram came from here. This is where he was doing his business. Now finding you here I suppose his business was to find you. You need to come home though. I need you closer and you need not worry about your father. In one of his tirades he collapsed and has been bedridden since. He is no longer in complete and total control of his business or his life. His precious name will vanish if you don't take it up again and I am sure I can convince him of that. Our solicitor convinced him of having things placed into my name to protect his holdings. We had papers drawn up that states him as still having control of business decisions but if such a time should arise where he is no longer able to make such decisions then it will fall to me. So you see you can come back home; or at least live closer to us."

"O mother, my practice is here. I can visit often though. You said William married. What became of his wife? Is she not still with you?"

"No Ashley left without a single word and seems to have vanished. That is what brought me here. I thought she might be trying to find out what actually happened to William. It is very upsetting as she was due to have a baby in May and the baby would have been the only connection to William our family would have had; the heir to Williams inheritance and if a boy would also carry the Radcliff name. She obviously knew Willard didn't approve of her. That's the only thing I can think of that would cause her to deprive us of our grandchild."

Denley managed to contain himself when he caught her name. Perhaps it's just a coincidence and they are two separate Ashley's, after all she introduced herself as Ashley Grey. That was not too likely though. But Ashley didn't seem to be the kind of person that would hurt a person like that. To withhold their grandchild from them after them loosing William was inexcusable. Things started clicking in when he remembered her arrival and going into labor early, their visit to Rosie Boyle's home now seemed to have significance. "Oh no," he moaned. "Mother I'll get you settled and then I have a house call to make. Can we meet for lunch at; say 1:00 at the tea house just down the street. I'll take the rest of the day off and we can catch up on everything else then."

"I'm already settled in at the hotel. I would like to check out some of the shops and freshen up. Promise you'll meet me and I'll let you do your call."

"I promise." Taking her by the hand he led her out into the street, gave her a kiss on the cheek and turned toward his carriage. The thoughts that were spinning in his head wouldn't stop and he couldn't get to Ashley's quick enough and to think that he had started to care for her. But he should hear her side of the story. No there was no excuse for doing such a thing. Leaving and giving them no opportunity to see their only grand child. He didn't even think Ashley was capable of such a hateful thing. Maybe he didn't know her as well as he thought he did. He was getting sick just thinking about it. He flicked the reigns to get the horse going faster. Standing at the door he smoothed his suit down and rapped on the door. After a polite greeting to Ellen he asked if he might have a word with Ashley in private.

Ashley entered the study with a smile on her face that was quickly replaced with concern when she noticed Denley's expression. "What a surprise to see you this morning. I was just telling Elizabeth about the beautiful pin you concealed with my hat; thank-you so much for it."

"Spare me your thanks and tell me what sort of game you're playing?"

"I haven't the faintest idea what you're talking about. Denley, what's going on?"

"Have you found what your looking for or are you intent on making me out to be a fool; Ashley Grey or should I say Radcliff?" He glared at her as if defying her to say anything. "You can't even deny it, can you?"

"How can you possibly know? The only person I've told was Elizabeth and that was in confidence."

"William was my brother." He almost spat the words out at her. "Yes that's right, my name is Denley Radcliff. He grabbed her arm, "I'll ask again; what sort of game are you playing? You've denied my Father and Mother the right to know their granddaughter. My mother found me and I've been told the whole story. You're sneaking off with out as much as a word. You've even been going by the last name Grey so you would be almost impossible to find."

Ashley pulling her arm free covered her face and began to cry. "I'm so sorry about William. But it's not as you think. I was looking for Denny; well I never imagined it was you. Not for a second. Please sit and I'll explain everything. I had planned to tell you everything this Saturday but not because I had figured any of this out."

"I'm not sitting to listen to more stories. I have to get out of here. I'll be late; I'm meeting Mother for tea so she can fill me in on the rest. I will disclose to her our interesting little conversation. I'm sure she'll be pleased to know the well being of her granddaughter even if she's not to be a part of her life." He turned on his heels allowing no more to be said and left the house in a hurry.

Ashley was standing in the middle of the study visibly shaken when Elizabeth walked in. Seeing her state she gathered her into her arms and gave her a shoulder to cry on. "I gather Denley is who you've been looking for all along. I'm sorry dear, but he spoke pretty loudly and I'm afraid all the staff heard too."

"He wouldn't even let me explain. He'll hear everything his mother has to say and it will only make me look worse."

"Give him time to think things over. When he's had time to cool down he may be willing to give you a chance."

"No, I don't think so but maybe it's time for Pauline to meet her granddaughter face to face. May I borrow the carriage to go into town?"

"Of course you may. You best hurry if you're going to try meeting them at the Tea House."

Ashley rushed out of the room and up the stairs. Asking Maggie to dress Katie in the new dress she rushed into her room and quickly changed and freshened her face a bit to cover the fact that she had been crying. Wrapping the pin up, she would return it to Denley before leaving. "Maggie would you be a dear and come along in the carriage to help with Katie?" Ashley didn't wait for a response. She already knew Maggie would be willing. She liked the outings to town.

Arriving at the Tea House not long after Pauline and Denley had ordered lunch Ashley excused Maggie and told her she would meet up with her later. Now straightening Katie's dress and smoothing out hers she looked in through the windows to see if she could spot their table and much to her relief they were still sitting over in a corner. Denley's back was to the door so that would give her an advantage. It would be a bit secluded and a little more private there. Summing up all her nerves she walked in and towards the table. Pauline hadn't noticed her until she was almost facing her.

"Mrs. Radcliff; how nice to see you again. Denley, I mean Mr. Radcliff was kind enough to inform me of your presence in town and I thought it would be an appropriate time to introduce you to your granddaughter. This is Katlaina Elizabeth Radcliff." She turned to Katie, "This is your grandmother sweetie. Do you have a hug for your grandmother?" Then she politely handed Katie over to Pauline.

Pauline's eyes began to glisten with joy as she reached out with her arms to hold her and receive the hug.

Denley was glaring at Ashley but had to change his expression quickly as Katie turned and held out her arms to him. He couldn't resist scooping her into his arms in his usual way and smiling at her. Pauline was a stranger to her and she didn't want to stay long on her lap. The bond these two seemed to have did not go unnoticed by Pauline as she sat back and watched.

The waitress brought another chair for Ashley to sit on and she declined ordering anything. "I don't want to intrude on your lunch. You probably have a lot to catch up on."

"Don't be daft. I've just met my granddaughter and I have some catching up to do with her as well." Then, turning to the waitress, "Please bring her a cup of tea and an egg salad sandwich." I hope that will be fine. It's what we've ordered.

"Is Mr. Radcliff in town as well?"

"No he's taken ill and is bed ridden. The doctor has ordered him remain calm and he doesn't know I'm here. But please tell me about Katie and how you've been doing."

They continued to chat politely all the while Pauline was watching Katie with Denley. They were too familiar with each other for it to be a doctor/patient relationship and Pauline was waiting for Denley to return to the conversation before asking about it.

Finally when she could stand it no more she turned to Denley, "Katie seems quite comfortable with you. I must assume that you and Ashley are more than acquaintances." Much to Ashley's relief the sandwiches were served before that could be answered and she wasn't sure what he would have said. She decided to finish lunch and excuse herself before the conversation came around to that again.

When she stood to leave Denley stood and carried Katie out to the carriage. "What are you up to?"

"Had you stayed long enough to listen to me you would have found I had no intention on keeping Katie from your parents. I was looking for you hoping to reconcile your differences with them so she could have a chance to know the rest of her family. You decided to think the worst of me though." She handed him the tissue with the pin tucked neatly in it and took Katie. "If your mother wishes to see Katie again before she leaves she is welcome to come by and spend time with her. Good day Mr. Radcliff." She had hoped calling him by his name would sting a little, after all hadn't he accused her of not disclosing her true identity.

She walked away from him without looking back and left him looking at the trinket he was holding and feeling somewhat of a heel. He should have given her the chance to explain and now it was too late. He slipped it into his pocket and returned to the table where his mother sat sipping her tea.

His mood change hadn't gone unnoticed by his mother, "I'm thinking you and Ashley must have gotten to be more than friends by Katie's response to you but by your appearance I have a feeling things are not too smooth at the moment. Is your attachment because of William?"

"No it has nothing to do with William. I didn't know she had been married to him until today. She has been going by the last name Grey and I assumed she was looking for a Denny Grey. I have only gone by Denley here. I paid her a visit earlier today and I refused to allow her to explain. With the way I talked to her and the words I said there will be nothing left to salvage. Ashley has given you permission to visit Katie if you would like to spend time getting to know her before you leave. I can make the necessary arrangements for you. Now, to change the subject, please tell me how you have been."

By the time Ashley arrived home she had calmed down and joined Elizabeth in the garden. Maggie offered to change Katie so she could join them and play with Snowball.

Over the next few days Mrs. Radcliff visited bearing gifts for Katie and tried to find out if there would be any chance of getting the two of them together to talk things out, but Ashley was not talking about it and avoided any conversation that went in that direction. Mrs. Radcliff knew her son Denny was miserable at work and at home and Ashley didn't look too happy either. She couldn't help but feel a bit to blame. Had she not arrived perhaps they would still be talking. Sooner or later they would have found out who each other was but under different circumstances they might have listened to each other. All Mrs. Radcliff knew is she was going to have to get them talking before she left, and that was soon. Realizing it was going to take drastic measures she decided a twisted ankle would be easy to pass off and so standing up she took a couple of steps and dropped to her knees pretending to be in agony. "It's my ankle; I've twisted it again. It hasn't been the same since I injured it some time ago. You remember Ashley when I did it just before you left. It feels bad. I need a doctor to look at it. I think you should send for Denny."

Maggie helped her to the couch and they propped her foot up. The stable hand was told to fetch Dr. Denley; that his mother was hurt, and the rest fussed over her to keep her comfortable until he arrived. She didn't mind the attention though she was feeling a bit guilty. She had gotten on well with Elizabeth and had hoped Elizabeth would not be angry if she knew she wasn't really hurt.

Ashley was just putting a cold cloth on it when Denley arrived and she took him aside quickly to tell him of her previous injury.

He poked and felt around the ankle and squeezed a bit and poked a bit more and shook his head, "I don't see any swelling or bruising. It seems fine but I'll wrap it up to support it a bit. Maybe you just irritated it; you have been overdoing things lately."

When he was finished wrapping her ankle Maggie put Katie down and she rushed over to Denley and she wrapped her arms around his neck to get the attention she was so used to receiving. He was just about to offer his mother a ride home when Ellen entered with a tray of goodies and tea. She poured the tea and left the room with Maggie following. They were sure this was a trick to get Denley to the house and decided an audience wouldn't be wanted. Elizabeth seemed to follow suit and made an excuse to attend to something in the kitchen.

Mrs. Radcliff now turned to Ashley and Denley, "Now that I've got you two in the same house you can either talk it out in front of Katie and myself or you can go to another room and talk things out privately; but it is obvious you two need to talk."

Denley handed Katie over to his mother and Ashley led the way into the study. Pouring two drinks Denley handed one to Ashley and then sat across from her. "Ashley I was so wrong in not letting you explain your side of the story. I want to know everything and I want to know why you went to so much trouble to keep Katie away from my parents and yet you were willing to bring Katie to the Tea house and introduce them. I want to know why your last name was kept secret."

Ashley began telling him the whole story and the more she said the more it made sense. He could picture his mother taking control. That is what she did his entire life and that is what she did this evening. The more Ashley went on with her explanation, the smaller Denley felt. "I have no more secrets left to tell. But it's your turn now. You don't use your last name and had you been using it I would have found you that first day Elizabeth brought you in to examine my condition. I had not intended to keep it a secret from Denny Radcliff."

"Yes it is my turn but first I need to apologize. I hope when I grabbed your arm I didn't hurt you."

"Apology accepted, and it did hurt, but mostly my feelings." She instinctively put her hand over her arm remembering how he had grabbed it.

"I turned out to be a disappointment to my father when I chose to practice medicine on patients of all classes. It disgusted him that I would lower my standards to treat the poor. I had watched all my life the way servants were talked down to and treated and how the poor were despised. He sent me off to school to have me molded the way he wanted but I had no intention of becoming him. William was the oldest and father always favored him anyway. Father didn't want me to destroy the Radcliff name so I dropped it. I packed my bags and walked away. I had no idea mother had taken it so badly. She didn't try to stop father, but then no one stopped father. I guess she figured I would at least stay close. That's another reason why it didn't work out between Sarah and me. I told you we were from two different worlds. She abhorred going into the poor end of town and I wasn't prepared to change for her when I had refused to change for father. I enjoy my practice here and the people need me. I was privileged to meet you here but I guess I am also to blame for you loosing your husband. William wouldn't have been here looking for me if I had stayed in contact with mother. That sounds bad for me doesn't it? I hope you don't hold that against me."

"No, it's done and can't be undone. It's just how circumstances turn out. I think William would have approved of you caring for Katie the way you do." Not wanting to say more she quickly turned her face from him and said they should return to the living room and check on his mother.

They returned to the living room to find the couch empty except for the bandage that had been wrapped around Mrs. Radcliff's ankle. They both gave a little chuckle and Denley just shook his head not surprised. "Was any of the ankle story this afternoon true?

"Apparently only the part I told you about her injuring it just before I came here."

They headed for the kitchen with Denley leading Ashley by the elbow like a true gentleman and there was Mrs. Radcliff standing at the cookie jar sneaking one for her little granddaughter Katie. "OK you caught me but everyone thought it was worth the trouble to get you here, though I did hurt my knee when I pretended to twist my ankle. Everyone erupted in laughter and even though Katie didn't know what was funny she started to giggle with everyone else.

8
A Cruel Man

The evening before Mrs. Radcliff was to board the carriage for her journey home Denley invited Ashley and of course Katie to join them for dinner. Ashley finally had the opportunity to wear the rose colored dress she purchased and Katie was wearing a new dress from her grandmother.

When Denley arrived to pick them up he couldn't believe how lucky he was to have a second chance. He owed his mother a huge thank you. He would have been terribly hurt to lose Ashley but he had also grown so fond of Katie. He was determined to look after the two of them if Ashley would allow it. William would have wanted it that way. It did seem a funny situation but he was going to propose to Ashley and offer her the name she already possessed. Not tonight though. Tonight was a celebration of having his family united; well almost. He would have to take a trip to Newcastle and see his father. Hopefully he will have softened after all this time.

Escorting Ashley out of the house by the hand and Katie insisting Denley carry her they made their way to the coach and sitting Katie in the coach he turned to help Ashley. "I was hoping you would wear that dress. You look beautiful in it but it is missing something. This I believe I already gave to you once before." He produced the pin wrapped in the tissue paper and handed it to her to pin to her dress. "But this I went back for after I had made the biggest fool of myself and you accepted my apology." With that he reached into his pocket and pulled out the matching necklace. He reached around her neck and did the clasp up and allowed his hands to linger on her neck a few seconds while he looked into her eyes. They didn't seem to hold the sadness they had before and yet she still looked so vulnerable. He kissed her very softly on the cheek before dropping his hands down to take hold of hers and help her into the carriage. Ashley felt as though she floated through the rest of the evening. All that mattered was Denley was smiling at her again, Mrs. Radcliff had finally met her granddaughter, and Ashley was no longer looking over her shoulder. The only obstacle left was Mr. Radcliff.

Denley helped his mother board the coach early the next morning with promises made to make a trip to Newcastle in the near future and to be sure to send letters between now and then. Ashley too had been made to promise to send letters, and she hoped Ashley would make the trip to introduce Katie to her grandfather as well.

As happy as Elizabeth was for Ashley she couldn't help but feel she may loose her and Katie and she had grown so attached to Katie she knew it was going to hurt. Ashley was expecting everything to fall back into place again but recognized some changes in Elizabeth. Finally one morning sitting in the garden having tea she asked Elizabeth what was wrong and Elizabeth had to tell her what was weighing on her mind.

"This will always be home for me and Katie. You are family now and nothing will ever change that. I could never tear Katie away from you.

With those words spoken everything did get back to normal; almost. The only exception is that Denley would be visiting much more often.

Mrs. Radcliff hadn't been gone a full month when Denley received word from her that his father had taken a turn for the worse and it would be advisable to come as soon as possible. She also requested him to invite Ashley and Katie along as this may be the only opportunity for him to meet his granddaughter.

Sitting beside Ashley, Denley showed her the letter. "I promised mother I would try to come after the heat of summer but it looks like I will be planning the trip even sooner. Do you think Ashley that you and Katie would be able to accompany me on the trip? If father isn't expected to live much longer as mother indicates it would be nice for him to meet Katie."

"Yes of course we should go as well. When do you plan to leave?"

"We should try to board the coach tomorrow after lunch and hopefully it will connect with the train without too much of a waiting time. I have made arrangements for another doctor to cover for me and he will be arriving on the morning coach. He has a sister in town he comes to visit every so often and he will stay with her. I will take him on my rounds and be by for you when I'm finished. I know; I have it all planned but I was hoping you would agree to come along. I should be on my way as I'm sure you will have plenty to do to prepare for the trip tomorrow."

Katie was used to coach rides. Not coaches as big, and not rides that took so long but she handled it well keeping Denley occupied. There were shades that were pulled down to keep some of the dust out and not being able to see where they were going was a little un-nerving.

The train ride was something totally new though. Denley went and bought the tickets while Ashley and Katie sat in the station house waiting for the train. When it finally drew close the train master pulled on the cord to make the whistle blow and Katie began to cry in fear. Ashley quickly soothed her and reassured her. Steam poured out of the chimney stack and the air took on a different smell. They waited as people stepped down onto the wooden platform and finally they heard the call, "All aboard!" She was getting very excited when Denley helped Ashley up and then carried her onto the waiting train. The seats were a padded dark green but would by no means be comfortable for long.

The whistle blew again and with a few slight jerks they could feel the train start moving and gradually picking up speed. Katie sat watching out the window as they moved along the track so quickly. The excitement turned into boredom and then she began fussing. It was a relief to both of them as the train drew closer and Katie finally fell asleep.

It was quite late when they arrived and Mrs. Radcliff had sent a coach to meet them. She had stayed up late to greet them and see to it that they were settled into their rooms.

Denley was given his old room and it hadn't been changed the whole time he had been gone.

Ashley had been given a different room than the one she had shared with William but supposed Mrs. Radcliff had done that so that Ashley wouldn't be troubled, and a small bed was set up in the same room for Katie. Denley gently settled Katie into the bed prepared for her and she snuggled right down and back to sleep.

The three of them tip-toed out and down to the sitting room for a night-cap and Mrs. Radcliff filled them in on Mr. Radcliff's condition. "I don't want to wake him tonight. Tomorrow will be a big enough shock for him to handle. He has no idea of your presence let alone the rest of the surprise in store for him. Finishing their drinks they all headed in their different directions for bed. Ashley was so exhausted but a little overwhelmed at being in this house again. She was grateful that she was able to surrender to the sleep she needed after being tired out by Katie.

Denley had a problem sleeping, as his last conversation with his father kept running through his head. There were some very hurtful words spoken between them and Denley wasn't without speaking his mind at the time either. He wasn't sure how it was going to go over with his father in the morning. Along with the fact that this was the first time he was spending the night under the same roof only a few rooms away from Ashley. Sleep was definitely not coming easy for him.

By morning Ashley and Katie had looked like they were well rested. Denley on the other hand looked like he hadn't slept a wink. They joined Mrs. Radcliff for breakfast before going in to see Mr. Radcliff. It was decided that Ashley would go in with Katie first and see if that softened him up a bit and so Mrs. Radcliff leading the way carried Katie in and introduced her to her grandfather.

"Well this is a surprise. I had assumed I would never meet my grandchild but I suppose with me knocking on deaths door the family returns for their inheritance. You picked a very convenient time to return."

Ashley face paled and she scooped Katie up away from him and walked out as quickly as she could to get away from this vile man that seemed to have no desire to love or be loved.

Mrs. Radcliff interrupted with a scolding tongue, "Willard! I finally get a chance to repair damage to an already fragile situation and how dare you drive them away. I invited her to come as our guest and to allow you a chance to finally meet your granddaughter; Williams only child."

Denley stood just outside the door listening to the whole conversation. He quickly took hold of Ashley's arm while she was trying to make her leave and asked her to please wait in the parlor for him. "I think perhaps we have made this trip for nothing but give me a few moments. I'll have mother join you."

Mrs. Radcliff had barely finished her sentence and Denley burst into the room to confront his father face to face. "Mother, go after Ashley in the parlor and sit with her please."

"Well it seems I'm to receive another surprise as if the first one wasn't enough. What are you doing in this house?"

"Poor father!" Denley almost spat the words out. "I don't expect you to treat me any different than you always have but to treat Ashley and your grand-daughter with such contempt…you have some nerve. I am surprised anyone has stayed with you over the years. You couldn't turn me into you so you turned me out. Did it give you some sort of satisfaction when you almost destroyed mother in the process. I had hoped you had changed but I can see you aren't capable of changing. You're an old fool and Ashley, Katie and I will not bother you with our presence in your room but we will remain in this house at Mothers wishes. But before I leave, you ought to know I intend to marry Ashley if she'll have me. I know in your opinion she wasn't good enough for William and I don't deserve someone as wonderful as her, but Katie is Williams daughter and carries the Radcliff name from William not me. So if I were you I would think long and hard about everything before you chase anyone willing to try to love you away. You will die a lonely old man even estranging your own wife and for what then have you worked your entire life for if you have nothing and no one to show for it in the end?"

In a rage Mr. Radcliff yelled at Denley as he was exiting the room, "You were never my son. You ask your mother who you belong to. Maybe she'll tell you the truth after all these years. You ask her!"

Denley's steps faltered for a second absorbing everything he just heard, then continued to the parlor. Did this information explain his father's feelings toward him all these years?

Ashley stood as he entered, "do you want to talk privately with Denley? I can take Katie to the kitchen for a bite before I put her down for a nap."

"No, that won't be necessary; anything we have to say can be addressed with you present. Sit back down dear and I'll ring for tea and a tray of snacks. I enjoy watching Katie play," Mrs. Radcliff said.

In the parlor he sat staring at his mother until he finally summoned the courage to ask the dreaded question. "Explain to me what father meant when he said I'm not his son. That maybe after all these years you would tell the truth. He told me to ask you; so I'm asking now?"

"Denley I have never been untrue with your father in all our years. All these years I have begged him to believe that, and now I am begging you to believe me. Your father never wanted any more children after William and to make sure of that he demanded we have separate sleeping arrangements but he was drunk one night and doesn't remember, well you can figure out what happened. We weren't getting along too well due to the situation so I took William with me and we went home to my mothers. I told him she needed help and I needed some time away to sort things out. I returned after you were born and he accused me of having an affair while I was gone and now I had come home to rub his face in it. You would carry his name but only to save his reputation. I tried to fuss over you to make up for the way he treated you. He accused me of giving you more attention to make up for you not getting to know your 'real father'. He always did things with William and despised your very existence. At times I thought of taking both you boys and leaving, but boys need a father. All these years he refused to believe me, and that is why he would tell you, you were a disappointment to him and you were going to destroy his precious family name. That is why he was so intent on pushing you away every chance he could. I tried to protect you from his hatred and the only reason he never told you that before was because William loved you so much he didn't want William to choose you over him."

"That explains so much over the years. It all makes sense now. As for my dear father I told him we were not leaving as we are here at your request but we will not enter his room again." Now turning to Ashley, "I hope that is alright with you Ashley? I am hoping that you will stay here and visit with mother until I tend to a few matters and make arrangements to go back home."

"Please dear do stay a little longer." Mrs. Radcliff joined in. "There is also a delicate matter we need to deal with while you're here. We do need to go through the room that William and you shared when you were last here. It hasn't been touched since you left but I imagine there are things in it that you may want that were Williams as well as things of yours you left behind. If you want to do it with someone present either Denley or I can help you, or you can do it privately if you wish. If you're not able to this visit it can wait but eventually you will have to do it."

Ashley sat looking down at her fingers to avoid eye contact but eventually replied. "Yes; yes I suppose I should attend to it. It would be good to have it done and behind me. I'll start into it first thing tomorrow." The rest of the day seemed a blur. It seemed impossible to get Mr. Radcliff's hateful words out of their minds. Of course Denley believed his mother but Ashley could see the pain in his eyes when she looked at him; especially if he didn't think anyone was looking. That evening when everyone seemed to be retiring it was with the exception of Denley.

He disappeared into the library and closed the door. Pouring a drink for himself and keeping the bottle close at hand he began going over in his mind all the terrible things his father had done to him over the years. Everything was explained this morning.

His father would take William riding and Denley had to stay; he didn't deserve a horse of his own, bad boys weren't rewarded with gifts. William could do no wrong but Denley was always wrong, always corrected, always punished for the smallest of things.

Denley poured himself another drink as he remembered a trip his father was planning. William of course was going and asked if Denley would be allowed to come too. It depended on whether Denley could behave which he doubted and Denley remembered he had been on his best behavior over the next few days. The night before the trip his father came into his room and told him he would have to stay home and get the mess in his bedroom in order. Except for one toy he had left out, his room was in perfect order. He remembered crying himself to sleep that night. When his father arranged to send him to boarding school he told him not to bother coming home for the holidays but to use the time to reflect on his life and behavior. To use the time to study and if he applied himself and worked hard at it maybe, just maybe he would be able to make something of himself. Denley had always thought it was to mold him into what his father expected him to be but now it was so plain. His father couldn't stand the sight of him let alone his closeness with his mother. That's why he pushed him to the limit. He wanted Denley to disappear.

Downing that drink he poured yet another one. Reflecting on the tears he shed in his younger years when he tried so hard to gain his fathers approval. But it wasn't about that and he would have never succeeded. He knew that now and he knew why, it wasn't because he was bad, it had nothing to do with that. He was punished because he didn't believe the Radcliff blood flowed in his veins. It was no wonder his mother never left him home with his father when she went out. She always told him when they went anywhere that it was their special time. She tried to do things with him to make up for the pain his father had caused.

By the time Denley finally stumbled up to his bed it was extremely late and he had also downed the whole bottle. He didn't believe in drinking his problems away but tonight it felt so good. Passing Ashley's door he paused when he noticed a candle light flickering and guessed Katie had woke up. He would have loved to say goodnight but figured it best Ashley not see him in the state he was. He made his way past her room and continued down the hall till he reached his room. He fell asleep on his bed still dressed and didn't move till late morning.

Ashley had not seen anything of Denley and was getting a bit concerned especially after yesterday's revelations. After breakfast she entered the room she had shared with William and decided to go through her things first. She kept the door open just in case Denley happened to walk by but she got absorbed in her task at hand and didn't notice if he had gone by or not. Looking through all the dresses she decided to donate them to the poor. She couldn't possibly wear them now. They were purchased to wear for William and it wouldn't seem right to wear them for Denley. She had started to purchase a new wardrobe and really didn't need too many more. Some of these dresses would be too large for her anyhow. They were bought because she was pregnant. She kept a few things that she had before she met William and they didn't seem to hold the same sentiment.

She had a few pieces of jewelry that were her mothers and of course she would keep them. In amongst them were a few special hat pins and hair pins and her mother's wedding band. Oh how she missed her mother and father. They have been gone for so long she hardly remembered them anymore. They died saving her from a fire that consumed their home. How she survived no one seemed to know but her aunt was willing to raise her up proper and she did her best to keep the memories of them alive. There were a few things she had purchased for a baby but now they would never fit Katie so she boxed them up too. She had three wooden boxes set by the door to go and she was almost finished her belongings when Katie began to fuss and so she tended to her and settled her down for a nap before going downstairs. When she left her room Denley was just coming out of his room and from what Ashley saw he looked rough. She couldn't help but feel for him. The blow he received had to be extremely devastating. She waited for him to close the distance between them and they walked down together. No words were spoken but Ashley could tell he felt a little embarrassed by his appearance. She knew he had been up late drinking. She had heard him pause briefly as he passed her door when she was up tending to Katie during the night. At the bottom of the stairs she gave his arm a gentle touch just to let him know she was there for him. It might be best to give him his space today if he wanted.

Tomorrow she would tackle Williams's belongings. Maybe if Denley felt up to it he would like go through it with her and pick a few of Williams's things to remember him by; she really didn't want to go through William's things by herself. If Denley was with her she might not relive every moment of their short time together with each piece she picked up. Denley would be able to keep her distracted and hopefully less emotional.

Denley didn't keep his distance like Ashley thought he might but he did seem a bit uncomfortable about his rugged appearance at first.

Katie had to feel Denley's whiskers on his face and it was comical to watch her reaction. By the time dinner had arrived though Denley had shaved and looked back to his normal self, but by the time dinner was over Ashley could feel one of her headaches coming on and she realized she hadn't had one in a long time. As she excused herself from the table Denley noticed Ashley was tensing up and offered a stroll in the gardens; maybe the fresh air would help, he knew he could use some fresh air too. He then excused himself and made his way around the table to escort her out toward the doors. "Mother would you mind tending to Katie for a bit." As they began to head out of doors he continued his conversation. "There are some very extensive gardens and ponds within the grounds that will be far more impressive now than when you would have been here in the fall and winter with William. I'm sorry. I shouldn't have mentioned his name. Because I had never seen you with him I sometimes forget the circumstances of your first visit here."

"Please don't apologize. He was a very important part of my life and without him I wouldn't have Katie. When my parents were killed I was raised by my aunt and she kept their memory alive so I wouldn't forget them. Even though Katie never met her father-no, more importantly because she never knew her father the only thing she will have is what she hears when we talk about him. I imagine how hard it was on my aunt but she left me a wealth of stories about my mother growing up and she shared what little she knew about my father. Sometimes I can't remember too much about being with them but I can close my eyes and see the stories she told me come alive. So when you hesitate over saying Williams name or feel guilty because you think you are bringing up sad memories for me, don't. Katie will learn more about William through you than she will ever learn through me. I want Katie to think of her dad as someone pleasant not a name we say in hushed words."

"Ashley you are an incredibly strong lady. For all you have been through you continue to surprise me." He took her by the hand and they continued to stroll along some of the paths. "I'm sure you know of my intentions toward you and I hope your feelings are the same toward me." He stopped walking and turned to face her and stroking her cheek with his hand he stared deep into her eyes. He kissed her very lightly and he could feel her warm inviting response and then wrapping his arms around her and pulling her even closer he kissed her again but with more intensity and she responded back matching his kiss. Then all of a sudden he pulled away and stepped back leaving her looking at him in disbelief. "I'm sorry. I have wanted to do that for so long but this is not the place."

They continued walking and Ashley snuggled into his arm a little closer. "I have a favor to ask of you. I have gone through all my things and they are boxed up to donate but I have William's belongings to go through and I was hoping you would be willing to sort through it with me. There may be things of sentimental value that you may treasure and want to keep. I think it will be easier for me too. I don't want to go through his things and relive all the memories we had. If you're there we can just get it done quickly; I hope."

"That I can help you with, but it will have to be in the afternoon. I have some things to tend to after breakfast."

"Will you be going in to town? I only ask because I have a letter I want sent out." "I can help you with that. If you have it ready just bring it down at breakfast tomorrow and I will be more than happy to send it off for you. Now how is your headache doing? Has the fresh air helped?"

"Maybe a little, but I did enjoy the stroll. I'm sure a good nights rest will help. We should return so I can get Katie tucked into bed."

By the time Ashley finally blew out the candles in her room she couldn't help but lay in bed going over in her mind the walk in the gardens, the conversation and the kiss that went with it.

She smiled inwardly. She could really be happy with him and she knew he would protect her to the best of his ability. He would care for Katie as if she were his own. The only thing that bothered her was the fact that with her he may never father children of his own and he is so good with Katie that he seemed the type of man that would want more children; especially children of his own.

At 3:00 am Mr. Radcliff rang his bell and was in distress. Denley flew down the stairs with his medical bag and headed for the door. Mrs. Radcliff was rushing out of her room and bumped into Ashley and so they headed down together clutching each others hands. They made their way down the stairs a little slower than Denley had and when they made it into the room Denley was trying to get some laudanum into his father to help with the pain. He seemed to be suffering from extreme pain in his chest from an old injury and was having trouble breathing. Finally his father's head collapsed back onto the pillow and his breathing began to return to normal. Denley listened to his lungs with his stethoscope and sat on the edge of the bed by his father until he fell asleep then he settled into a large comfortable over stuffed chair and fell asleep himself.

Denley didn't emerge from his room until after 10:00 am and when he did come out you couldn't miss the tears in his eyes. Immediately Mrs. Radcliff began to cry thinking the worst and Denley quickly responded "Father is awake and is calling for you mother." The words came out almost choked like it was hard to speak and Mrs. Radcliff looked to him immediately thinking of the horrible words spoken to him only a couple of days ago and hoping it was not repeated especially after all Denley had done for him in the wee hours of the morning. "It's ok mother." You could hear the raw emotion in his voice that made it difficult to speak, "Everything is better than ok. Father asked me to forgive him for treating me so harshly over the years and wishes he could undo all the hurt he has caused. He wants to be surrounded by his family. He also apologized for the other day and told me he had no right to speak to Ashley the way he had and wants to meet his grand daughter. He wants to speak to you first and then he wants Ashley and Katie to come in to him."

Mrs. Radcliff dabbed at her eyes with a lace trimmed hankie as she turned to go in and as she sat on the side of his bed he held her hand for the first time in years. In tears he began, "I have been a fool all these years and nobody could stop me. I know you were never unfaithful to me. I was too proud to admit it by then because if I did that then I would have to believe my actions toward you the night I got drunk were reprehensible. I don't remember that night but from what you told me that next day and the look of hurt you had on your face I am ashamed and so sorry. I only hope you can forgive me."

Pauline bent over and gave Willard a gentle hug and wiped her eyes again. She too found it hard to speak, feeling choked. By the time she left the room Denley had carried Katie to the door and was waiting to go back in with Ashley by his side.

"Please Ashley come closer," he said holding out his hand as she stopped just inside the door. With a slight hesitation she then moved closer and took his big outstretched hand in hers. "I apologize for the terrible accusation I made to you the other day and I only hope you can forgive an old fool. I also apologize for the way I treated you and made you feel when William brought you here to introduce you to the rest of the family. I am sorry for the loss you suffered that because of me may have been avoided and I can not undo things but you seem to have found a place in Denley's heart and you have my blessings. Now may I see my granddaughter?"

Denley now smiling brought Katie forward and he released Ashley's hand to receive a quick hug from Katie. Over the course of the next two weeks everyone spent a great deal of time in Mr. Radcliff's room and slowly Katie became more comfortable around him as he enjoyed her entertaining ways. Denley was making up for lost time forging a new relationship with his father who now seemed so different and Mrs. Radcliff was also enjoying the new Mr. Radcliff. The one she fell in love with so many years ago.

    Mr. Radcliff had another attack in the night and this time Denley was unable to bring him out of it.

9
After the Funeral

Somehow seeing Sarah at the funeral didn't entirely surprise Denley. While she had never met any of Denley's immediate family, he had disclosed his family name and that he was originally from Newcastle. Being engaged to Sarah he had also disclosed most of his family information. Because his father was the well known owner of a shipyard and was extremely well off, his death was big news. She had come on the pretense of paying her respects but was after so much more.

Walking back to the carriage with his mother and Ashley and carrying Katie, Sarah approached and asked for a moment of his time. He turned to his mother and Ashley, "I'll join you in the carriage in a moment." He handed Katie over to Ashley and they walked away from the group of friends that were working their way back to their carriages and some that had stopped at other grave sights to pay their respects to loved ones that had been buried there. Sarah looped her arm through his but because he was a gentle man and he wouldn't embarrass Sarah so publicly he waited to remove her arm until they were in a quiet place

Sarah looked appropriately saddened for the occasion but slightly annoyed when Denley unhooked his arm from hers. She tried to playfully tease Denley in hopes of rekindling their old relationship and she finally stood facing him with a small pout on her lips before speaking. "I am truly sorry for your loss Denley. I'm staying at the Royal Station Hotel in town. I would like it if you came to see me before I leave town. No doubt you will be busy with your solicitors but I would dearly love it if you stopped by for tea. I imagine if you and your brother are as close as you said, he will be sharing his inheritance with you. I didn't notice your brother with your family. As the sole beneficiary you would think he would have at least made an appearance."

Denley finally stopped her before she could say more. "My brother died over a year and a half ago. You have met the sole heir of the estate though."

A smile made its way across her face presuming he now had to be the heir. The look on her face gave him the impression she was calculating his worth but before she could respond he continued, "You'll no doubt remember a house call you came with me on and I introduced you to a young woman Ashley Grey; well as it turns out she was married to my brother. Her baby that I was checking on that day is Williams only child and bears the Radcliff name and she is the heir to the estate. Now if you'll excuse me I would like to wish you a good trip back to London and I am on my way back to the carriage. Just so you're clear on where we stand, I have happily moved on with my life and you should too. I am hoping to be engaged shortly and am very happy with how things have turned out. It seems you did me a big favor leaving me when you did and I believe I told you the last time I saw you that you saved us a lot of heart ache." To make sure she understood it was totally over with no chance of rekindling their relationship he said with finality, "Good bye Sarah."

He turned and walked away and paying no attention to anything else she was trying to say joined his mother and Ashley back at the waiting carriage where they were obviously deep in thought. Even though he had been in a quiet part of the cemetery with Sarah, they weren't out of sight from the carriage and his mother wanted to know who the young lady was that was trying so hard to get his affections. Picking Katie up to take her seat by Ashley he held her on his knee and after explaining the situation he motioned to the driver that they were ready to leave.

When they finally arrived back home and settled in Mrs. Radcliff then spoke up. "Denley tomorrow you and I have an appointment to visit the solicitor. There is the will to attend to and some company business I am hoping you will be able to help me sort through."

"Yes, I had figured that would be the case. I also need to start looking into the times for the train departures. I believe Ashley and Katie are getting ready for home."

"I am beginning to miss Elizabeth and Maggie but take the time you need to get things in order for your mother."

Mrs. Radcliff finally a bit exasperated corrected her, "Will you please call me mother or mother Pauline or even Pauline; at least something a little less formal than Mrs. Radcliff, or referring to me as 'your mother' when speaking to Denley."

"I am so sorry; I never even gave it a thought. I will try to remember to call you Mother Pauline; I like the sound of that. Now if you will excuse me I'll leave you both to make your plans for tomorrow and I want to put Katie down for a nap."

After tucking Katie in and closing the door she stood staring at the room her and William had shared. The daunting task of tending to William's personal belongings had been put off because they had been spending most of their time with Mr.…no Father Radcliff. Perhaps she could do it alone. She really didn't want to bother Denley with it now. He has been through so much turmoil since they arrived especially with his father dying. She walked over to the door and hesitated momentarily then, telling herself she was being silly about it walked in to start. She decided to set anything that might be sentimental on the bed for Denley to go through later. William had left some of his belongings in the trunk and when he had left looking for Denley she had put other things just on top to give her a bit more room while he was away. Pulling everything out and starting through them she started putting things aside to be donated. Then she came across a small parcel that had been unopened...

Denley came up looking for Ashley when she didn't join them downstairs and found her lying on the bed curled up and sobbing uncontrollably. He gave a light tap on the door and entered. Terribly concerned he approached and sat on the bed beside her and with a soft kind voice he put his hand on her shoulder to bring her around into his arms. "You should have told me you were going to go through the room today Ashley I would have helped you. What is so disturbing that it would put you into such a state?"

Without a word she handed him the small opened package with a note attached and he began to read:

My dearest Ashley:

This is such a small token of my complete love for you. It cannot compare to what you have given me. You have blessed me with the precious gift of your love, and now a gift that I cannot possibly ever come close to thanking you for. I look forward to the birth of our child.

Your loving husband always William

Within the package there was the small token spoken of in the letter. A gold ring with hearts engraved all around and a diamond set into the center of a larger heart.

Denley set it gently on a cabinet and pulled her closer into his arms.

"I was doing fine until I opened that. I was doing just fine," She sobbed.

He sat for the longest time just holding her in his arms stroking her hair and wishing he could take the pain away, but, feeling helpless he was only able to offer a hearing ear and a shoulder to cry on.

Then trying to pull herself together and wiping her eyes with a handkerchief Denley handed her, she continued, "I have it almost finished and anything you might want is here on the bed," she tried to sound more natural smoothing down her dress while avoiding his eyes. At that moment Katie let out a cry and thankful for the interruption she made her excuse to leave. As she was walking toward the door she told Denley to feel free to go through the things on the bed and everything left in the room that didn't belong to Mother Pauline he could donate to the poor.

Denley put the ring and the note in his pocket. It may be something Katie might want when she is old enough to appreciate the sentiment.

When Ashley finally made her way downstairs with Katie she snuck out the door and allowing Katie to walk they made their way into the garden where there was a comfortable bench. She sat and watched Katie chase a butterfly but she was troubled by Denley finding her in the room sobbing. What would he think seeing her fall apart like that? With the feelings he has for her it must hurt him that she still cries for William. Seeing that ring totally undid the wall she was trying to put up. It was a ring she had looked at one day shortly after they were married. He was busy looking at cuff links and she decided to try it on. She didn't realize William had even noticed. He would have had to go back on his own later to pick it up. He had to have kept it for some time waiting for a special moment to give it to her because she wasn't pregnant yet.

Denley was having tea with his mother and happened to notice Katie out in the garden and just off to the side, almost obscured by a flowering shrub sat Ashley. She looked lost and it hurt him to see her looking so vulnerable. He asked his mother to find an excuse to go and get Katie and then he went out and joined Ashley on the bench. She rested her head on his shoulder and they sat together quietly for some time before he finally spoke. "This has been an extremely difficult and emotional trip for you. You don't need to try and hide that." He took one of her hands and looking at her hand in his he continued, "If you need to talk, I'll listen. Would you like a bit of a stroll through the grounds? I would be more than willing to join you."

"I'm sorry for earlier. A stroll would be nice though."

"There is nothing to apologize for. I can't imagine how difficult the last few weeks have been on you. I just want you to know I'm here for you. If you need a shoulder to cry on that's ok, I wish I could take all that hurt away but I feel so helpless." They walked hand in hand around the grounds in silence for a bit and then slowly the conversation returned and her heart felt a little more at ease.

The next morning Mother Pauline and Denley had left the house early for their appointment with the solicitor. The reading of the will that Mr. Radcliff had drawn up always worried Pauline. The papers that were done up more recently were null because Mr. Radcliff had remained in full power over his business before he died. As they sat at the desk Mr. Sherman the solicitor cleared his throat before beginning. He was an older man with grey hair and blue smiling eyes. He had looked after the legal end of the Radcliff's business dealings for many years now.

He opened a large folder, cleared his throat again and began to read off the details.

Pauline's mouth dropped open and Denley was in shock. Finally when Pauline was able to speak she asked, "When were the changes made to the will? It is not the way Willard had told me it was written out. Mind you that was before William was killed."

He pulled out two envelopes and handed one to Denley and said that it was all explained within the letter. The second letter he handed to Pauline and told her it was to read in private, a personal letter from Mr. Radcliff. I have full knowledge of the contents of the letter and it is signed and dated.

As Denley scanned the contents of the first letter he realized that his father had intended on waiting until after his death to form an apology and the explanation for the way he felt. Had Denley not saved his fathers life with the first attack and slept in that overstuffed chair that night things may have been very different. As it was he was given the explanation and the apology personally and was able to form a bond with his father that was special even though it was all too quickly taken away. Denley finished reading it and then handed it to his mother to read. "Its date is around the time you came looking for me."

After Pauline finished reading the letter Mr. Sherman finally spoke again. "Mr. Radcliff had sent word to me about revising the will when you were out of town. He asked if I minded making a house call. He told me he didn't know where you were but he could guess and it turns out he was right. He thought you might go looking for your daughter-in-law and grand child and was hoping that might lead you to Mr.Denley Radcliff. If his suspicions turned out right he wanted to make sure everything was in order in the event that he didn't survive before your return."

Ms. Radcliff was left the house she resided in along with a few smaller local properties and she was to be cared for financially by Mr. Denley Radcliff. The shipyard along with other properties further from Newcastle was left to Denley along with a very large sum of money. In the event of finding Williams only child provisions were put in place for the education and adequate funds would be left over for a very comfortable living upon graduation including a share in the ship yard. Ashley was also left a modest allowance for her comfort and the raising of his grandchild. This too was no small amount.

His father seemed to cover everyone including his longtime butler, his stable hand Karl and any of the servants that were still under Ms. Radcliff's charge. All would receive a tidy bonus.

"I am hoping you keep me employed as your father did Mr. Radcliff. I am familiar with all of his holdings and the details of each property and I am confident that I will be of great assistance especially as you begin taking control of the shipyard."

Denley and Pauline decided to have a cup of tea before heading home and they sat looking out the window discussing the will when Sarah walked by. Quickly Denley turned his head hoping she wouldn't notice him, but she had. She seemed to get the point of their last discussion because she looked in his direction and then turning her nose up quickly continued past the door much to his relief.

When they arrived home Denley filled Ashley in on the provisions made for her and Katie and spent the rest of the afternoon going over books with his mother so that everything would be in order. His mother would keep in contact with him with regards to any decisions needing to be made with the ship yard. They would be boarding the train for home in two days and Pauline was putting on a bold face but she was going to miss them all terribly.

Their last full day arrived and Denley invited Ashley to bring Katie and meet him in the stables. The stables always seemed to be a gloomy place for Denley and he wanted to be out there first to shake off any of the negative effects, he also had much work to do. The stall that should have held his horse had he been given one as a young child was used for storage. With Karl, the stable hands help it was cleaned out and fresh straw was put down. There was a certain satisfaction in knowing that it would have a horse in it now as Denley felt all children should have a horse of their own. Karl was left to lead the filly into the stall and have her brushed down and hopefully calm by the time Ashley and Katie started down the cobbled path. Denley went out to meet them and scooped Katie up in the usual manner and led Ashley by her elbow down the path.

"I have a nice surprise for you Katie. Every little girl needs a pony of her own," he said as he was opening up the door to the stable. In a rush the filly flew out the door with Karl fast behind pausing only long enough to say she had spooked.

"Well so much for that." Pointing to the filly for the benefit of Katie, "There goes your little horse Katie. Next time you come you should be able to pet her." Then turning to Ashley he added, "Karl will be working with her to get her used to being handled and ridden. She'll be as gentle as a lamb by the time Katie is old enough to ride her. Karl is good with horses that way."

Karl was a shy young man of average height and slim build that had worked in the stables along with his father until his death and so Karl remained on, tending the horses and carriages and all that went with it. His father had taught him to be reliable and Pauline would not have to worry about that part of her property. Karl lived in a small secondary house on the property and if he ever married it would be of sufficient size to bring a wife.

They went into the stable and looked at the other horses and Katie was able to at least see some of the older ones. Just before they were going to go back to the house Karl led the filly back in and led her to her stall. Apologizing to Denley he commented that she had some spunk and wasn't used to the new stall. Then he went about brushing her down a bit.

The rest of the day was going to be a gloomy one for Pauline. With this being the last day before everyone would be leaving Pauline wanted to have a private moment with Ashley and took the opportunity when she spotted Ashley out sitting on a swing on the patio. Ordering a tray of tea and scones to be brought out she joined Ashley on the patio but sat facing her. "I'm not sure I've thanked you properly for coming with Denley. I don't suppose it was easy coming back here considering everything but I am so happy to have you and Katie in my life, and that Willard was able to see Katie before he died." She stopped to sip her tea.

"Mother Pauline, when I left it was never my intention to withhold Katie from you. I just had to sort some things out. I guess I panicked with the whole situation. I really hadn't got to know you that well and I felt like a stranger under a looking glass. It has turned out well, and I've enjoyed being here though the funeral we all could have done without. I am sorry about Mr. Radcliff"

"I am too. He changed so much in that last couple of weeks. I was just starting to get to know him all over again. I have noticed the growing attraction between you and Denley and I am happy for both of you. You look good together." Some words although unspoken were understood between both.

"I know he'll take good care of Katie and me. Somehow I think William would have approved."

"He'll make a wonderful father. I look forward to lots of little grandchildren running around this house when you come to visit.

I'm sorry; I'm getting way ahead of you. I am just too forward for my own good. Well I should go in and see if Katie is up from her nap yet. My time with her is running out for this visit."

Ashley remained sitting on the swing. Panic slowly gripping her as the full impact of what Pauline had just said sank in. He would make a wonderful father. He was the type of man that should have children; definitely more than one and especially of his own. How could she be responsible for depriving him of that? She really cared for him and it was going to hurt her to let him go but he would be thankful for the decision, not now, but when he is eventually holding his own children in his arms he'll understand. Making up her mind not to do anything before they arrived back home so the train ride would not be awkward or upsetting she headed back in to get things ready.

Denley had spent so much time looking over papers and deciding what he wanted to take home with him he hardly had time to visit let alone notice that Ashley's feelings toward him were slowly becoming less visible. Anything he might have noticed he put down to the death of his father, the funeral, and the desire to go back home. This shipyard and the other holdings his father left to him were going to take some time to get used to. William was the one that was supposed to inherit those things and he knew the business top to bottom but this was all foreign to Denley. The wealth that he was always denied but never missed was now his and there would be certain expectations he would have to live up to, but he did not want to let it affect who he was as a person.

His mother had snuck off with Katie to do some last minute shopping. She enjoyed spoiling Katie and he wouldn't be surprised to see his mother in Harwell within a few weeks. When Denley finally emerged into the main sitting room he realized he was alone. He sat in a big comfortable chair with his feet propped up and started to reflect on this whole visit: The change in his father before he died. Why couldn't the change have happened years ago? He hadn't had a chance to really get to know him. The closeness that he was developing even further with Ashley and seeing her with his mother warmed his heart. Even Katie was at ease here. It was so nice to be home and now already it was time to go. Slowly his eyelids closed and he didn't wake up until he felt Katie crawling up on his lap. This little girl certainly had him wrapped around her little finger. In so many ways he felt more like a father to her than anything else.

Just as he was opening his eyes Ashley was trying to take Katie off his lap without disturbing him. "I'm sorry, I tried to catch her but I was a bit distracted with all the parcels mother Pauline brought in, and she is getting very quick."

Straightening up in the chair and feeling a bit embarrassed that he was caught napping he got to his feet. "It's ok. I hadn't meant to fall asleep."

"I've been meaning to let you know I want to get off the train in Sheffield and stay for a couple of days. I have a dear friend there I haven't seen in probably four years now. It seems a shame to go right through when I know the train stops there. I would love for her to see my Katie too. She has two little girls and a boy now and I've only seen her oldest."

"Yes of course you should see her. Have you sent word to make sure she will be able to meet up with you?"

"Yes the letter you sent for me; well she sent a reply asking me to come. It was more her idea than mine. She said she is easy to find and she wouldn't take no for an answer. Would you mind terribly if I sent one of the trunks I brought with you to take to Elizabeth's. I don't need everything and I packed the things I need at Josie's separately? I'll send along a note for Elizabeth so she knows where I am if she should need to get in touch with me, but I will only be a couple of days. I am getting anxious to get home too."

"That won't be a problem but I might not get the trunk to Elizabeth's until the next day. I think I'll be arriving too late to deliver it immediately."

Pauline entered the room and asked if they were going to spend the rest of the day standing there talking or if they were going to include her in the conversation. "I'm losing all three of you tomorrow and it's going to be terribly lonely here." She sat down in a bit of a huff, "I wish you could stay longer: oh I know Denley you don't have to say it. You have your practice to get back to. I can wish though."

"With the shipyard and other properties to tend to now I'm sure we'll be seeing a lot of each other."

The remainder of the evening went by with the idle chatter of tomorrow and Ashley's plans. Some of the luggage was brought down and ready to be loaded in the morning.

"I won't be seeing you off tomorrow. It's too early but I've informed Karl of the time you need to leave by so he'll be here a little earlier to load the carriage. I've also asked the cook to prepare a couple of baskets of goodies for you take along.

They said there emotional good-byes before going to bed that evening and Ashley couldn't help but feel a bit sad for mother Pauline. Knowing she would be waking up to a quiet house and so many changes that have happened in so little time.

Katie didn't play Ashley out so much with the trip cut almost in half. Denley helped her with her luggage when they arrived in Sheffield. He had an hour before he had to board the train again.

Josie let out a squeal of excitement when she caught sight of Ashley and they rushed to meet giving each other a hug and kiss on each cheek. Ashley was equally excited to see Josie and Denley stood back and watched the two of them. Finally Ashley looked around and straightened, "Where are my manners. This is Denley Radcliff, I mentioned him in my letter, and this is my daughter Katie."

Offering her hand in greeting she lost her big smile and replaced it with a sympathetic look. "I'm sorry to have heard about your father but it is a pleasure to meet you," then acknowledging Katie clinging to Denley, "she's got your eyes Ashley." Her smile returned as she turned to her three shy children standing in a row behind her and pointing at each she introduced their names, "Maddie, Caroline, and Blaine." Grabbing Ashley's hand again, "We have so much to catch up on. Let's get your things onto the carriage."

Denley helped all four children up into the carriage and loaded Ashley's luggage into the back. "I should be getting back to the train and let you ladies be on your way." He took Josie by the hand to help her into the carriage and then walked around to the other side with Ashley and taking her by the hand to help her he quickly gave her a kiss on the cheek "I'll see you then in a couple of days. Enjoy your visit and I hope your train ride home is pleasant." Then he helped her up into her spot. He watched as they disappeared and then returned to the train and pulled some papers out to go over. There was something about the papers. He couldn't quite put his finger on it but he was determined to get to the bottom of it, and without the distraction of Katie's energy he would have plenty of time to try and find what he was looking for.

Josie had to comment immediately on Denley's attentiveness to Katie and give her approval. Ashley let the comments slide; she really didn't want to get into that conversation; at least not yet. They caught up on all the things that had taken place since they had last seen each other. Some of the experiences Ashley had been through left Josie speechless. When the children were finally all tucked in for the night and Josie's husband Charles was content for the evening Josie pushed for more details about Denley.

Giving in to her friends unending questions she finally revealed the details Josie had been waiting for all evening. They were the best of friends when they attended school together and were inseparable. By the time she was finished Josie could understand Ashley's thinking but did have some reservations. "You should give him the whole truth. He deserves that much."

"If I do that he'll try and talk me out of it. But he loves children and he should have some of his own. I don't want to be the one to take that away from him. He would hate me later and I couldn't bear to have that happen. It would be better to hurt a little now than a lot later."

By the time the couple of days had come to an end she was wishing she had planned a little longer but she also wanted to get home and back to normal. She was not looking forward to the conversation she needed to have with Denley and had gone over in her mind so many times what she was going to say and it always sounded so feeble.

10
An Unpleasant Conversation

Denley was waiting for Ashley and Katie when the coach finally came to a stop. It was so good to be on familiar ground again. Katie couldn't get into Denley's waiting arms quick enough and it hit Ashley as to how hard this was going to be on her. She had thought about how it was going to affect Denley and herself but Katie loved him too.

"You almost beat your trunk home. I only delivered it yesterday. I hope you had a nice visit with your friend. You two must have been quite close at one time."

"We went to school together and we were the best of friends. Some of the other girls called us the twins and we did have a nice time thank-you. I should have sent Katie home with you though. She was terrible coming home. But I think she just needs things back to normal again."

"Well let's not keep her waiting any longer."

When the horse was close enough to hear trotting down through the entrance Elizabeth rushed out onto the porch to greet them. Right behind her was Maggie and Ellen, and on their heels was Snowball. When the horse finally came to a stop Elizabeth was the first to speak as she was reaching for Katie, "Welcome back. I have missed you both so much. I was worried you might decide to stay in Sheffield. Denley told me it looked like you were very close friends."

"Elizabeth you made this home to us and that's not going to change unless you get tired of having us here."

"That I can assure you will never happen. So let's get inside, have some tea and you can tell us all about your trip."

Maggie helped Denley bring Ashley's luggage in and without an invitation to stay he said his good-byes and made an excuse to get back to work.

Ashley followed Denley outside and thanked him for being available to pick them up. She was trying to keep a little distance to avoid giving him the chance to sneak a kiss. Every time he kissed her it made the conversation she needed to have with him just a little harder and it was going to be hard enough as it was.

"Denley I need to talk to you about something. This isn't easy to say because I care about you but I've been thinking…" she paused to try and come up with the right words. "Since I fell apart after finding that ring in Williams's belongings…It made me realize that I'm not ready to take that step again." She watched the expression change on his face and she knew this hit him hard. "You'll find someone special and you'll thank me later. I don't want you to feel like your always standing in William's shadow, and he'll always be there. Right now you think it won't bother you but it would slowly gnaw at you. I couldn't bear the idea of putting either one of us through that. I…" She stopped, lost for words and stood looking at her fingers, afraid to look up at his face until he spoke.

"I can wait; I can give you all the time you need. Ashley, please don't do this. That moment we had in the garden was real and it was me that stopped it because it was the wrong time and place. Your reaction didn't say you needed more time."

"I don't want you waiting for me. Please Denley this is hard enough and Katie loves you. You're her uncle and she is still going to need to see you. We're still family just not the way you want it to be." She turned before he could see the tears well up in her eyes and she couldn't bear to see the pleading look on his face. Walking quickly into the house she darted up the stairs to her room and listened for the horse's hooves make the clickety-clack sound back out the drive. She stole a peek out the window but the vision was a blur through tear filled eyes. She had been thinking this through the last couple of days and as prepared as she thought she was she was wrong. All this time she had been telling herself Denley would be a good father and husband but she had never told herself she loved him. She sank down on her bed hugging a pillow.

Denley's horse trotted down the drive and Denley was trying to figure out what had just happened. He was so sure of his feelings for Ashley and he thought her feelings for him were the same. What changed? He had never considered being in Williams shadow but Ashley's perspective on things would be a bit different. Would she change her mind if he gave her time? What did she say? "I don't want you waiting for me." Those were her exact words. It was becoming very obvious that dating was not for him and remaining single would at least spare the heart ache he was feeling now.

When Ashley didn't come back down after she had seen Denley to the door Elizabeth went up and tapped on her door. She was let in by Ashley and by the look on Ashley's face she knew something had happened. She just wasn't sure if it happened in Newcastle or just before Denley left today. Maybe they had an argument in Newcastle and Denley wanted it settled before he left. She had asked Denley if he could meet Ashley at the coach and maybe that was a bad idea. "I'm sorry if I used bad judgment in having Denley meet you at the coach. I thought you would be happy to see him but it is obvious something has happened. You didn't invite him to stay for tea and you didn't stand close to him when he finished bringing your things in."

"No it's not your fault." Ashley told her most of the story but held back the comment that Pauline had made about all the grandchildren she was looking forward to having. Elizabeth didn't need to know that was the main reason. If she had told her that part Elizabeth might have felt she could help by telling Denley. She didn't want to take that chance. "Denley had no idea what was coming. I should have waited a day or two but I just wanted to get it over with and I didn't feel Newcastle was the best place to do it especially with the train ride home. Going to Sheffield was a good way of breaking the trip up and giving us a little distance."

She cried herself to sleep the next couple of nights when she recalled the desperate plea from him and she wanted so badly to hold him in her arms and forget the whole conversation. She tried so hard to put on a happy face during the days but she was sure Elizabeth knew something was wrong; that there was more to it than not being over William.

Telling herself they would eventually have to face one another especially because they were still related and Katie dearly loved Denley, she decided to just stop by and see how he was doing. She didn't have a very good excuse but they couldn't keep avoiding one another. Trying to stay away from the frills and lace that she usually wore she chose a simple dress that didn't attract too much attention.

Gathering all her nerves up and taking a few deep breaths she stepped down out of the carriage and paused in front of the door to his office. One more deep breath and she entered only to stand looking at a man probably in his early sixties with small smiling eyes, silver hair and a neatly kept silver mustache sitting at the desk. He was wearing a white over coat and he had a stethoscope hanging around his neck. He wasn't a tall man but he was well proportioned. She fumbled a bit not sure what to say as several thoughts went racing around in her head. "I'm sorry you have to forgive my manners, I just didn't realize Dr. Denley still had someone standing in for him. You must be Dr. John Kerrington. I'm Ashley Radcliff," she offered her hand in greeting, "and I was hoping to have a word with Dr. Denley."

"I'm pleased to meet you but I'm sorry I can't help you. I would like to have a word with Dr. Denley myself. I was supposed to be leaving today but he hasn't shown up for work now going on three days. The last time I saw him someone came for him just at closing time; he grabbed his bag and left with the man. I expected him back at least by the next morning but I haven't heard from him since. I don't know this town well enough to even go looking for him."

"Are you looking after any patients that might need an evening house call, someone in labor or did he give a name; anything?" She was grasping at straws but this was not like Denley at all. He took his practice very seriously.

"No, there is nothing I can tell you."

"I have to go. I have a place to check. A woman by the name of Rosie Boyle runs a boarding house and sometimes she gets someone in there needing medical help.

Dr. Kerrington grabbed for his medical bag, "I'm not letting you go by yourself. You may need my assistance or if that's where he is, he may need assistance." They both climbed into her small open carriage and she directed the horse down the street heading east.

Arriving in front of Rosie's, Ashley bailed out quickly and rushed up to the door. She immediately saw the Quarantine sign and banged on the door hoping someone could tell her what she needed to know. If Denley was in there treating patients it would explain everything.

Rosie came to the door but wouldn't open it. But speaking loudly enough to be heard, "I can't open the door to ya love. We might have the fever here. What is it your lookin for?"

"Is Dr. Denley in there Rosie? He's been missing for a few days now."

"Oh aye, he's here alright. But he's one of them that's got the fever."

Ashley's heart sank. By this time Dr. Kerrington was standing behind Ashley and he spoke up. "I've never been exposed to the fever. Mrs. Boyle how many are down with it in there?

"Two, Dr. Denley and the man he was brung in here to see. Dr. Denley treated him on the train. He didn't know on the train that he was dealin with the fever. They're both in a bad way if ya know what I mean. Especially the Larson feller, but he's not as young as Dr. Denley."

"Rosie you have to let me in. I've been exposed to the fever years ago and I'll be ok." "Dr Kerrington, you need to go back to my place and tell Elizabeth what is happening and ask her to please take care of Katie. She also might know of anyone else that's been exposed that will be able to help if this becomes a serious outbreak. Come back here after and I'll have a list ready for anything I need, and if you can think of anything helpful bring it along. Other than that the best thing you can do is take care of Dr. Denley's patients and be on the watch for any other signs of fever. You go before Rosie opens the door."

As he was climbing back into the carriage Rosie opened the door and Ashley quickly slipped in. Then she went into full gear. "Rosie I want you to have everything your using boiled. The rags you're using on the men need to be switched often and they can be boiled to clean them or burned. The water in the bowls by their beds needs to be changed often too. Are there any others that were staying here since Mr. Larson arrived?"

"No, not for a week till Mr. Larson came."

"Good, hopefully he didn't spread it on the train. Now please take me to Dr. Denley if he's alert enough he might be able to help me with a list. Can you bring me a scrap of paper and something to write with?"

Rosie led her into Denley's room and it took Ashley by surprise. He probably hadn't had a shave since the day she came back. She quietly whispered to Rosie to change the water and bring some fresh rags. Then she turned her attention to Denley, "Aren't you a terrible sight," she said softly as Rosie sat the fresh bowl of water down and handed her some rags. She plunged a rag into the cold water, wrung it out and dabbed Denley's face, forehead, and neck with it. "Goodness you're burning up". She repeated the procedure.

"Ashley you shouldn't have come," he moaned, "it's contagious. You shouldn't be here."

"I was exposed to the fever when I was younger."

"Have you checked on Mr. Larson yet?"

"Not yet, I want to make a list of things we need. Dr. Kerrington will be by for it in a bit. Can you think of anything? I'm thinking of Laudanum, and alcohol or something to use for cleaning, is there anything else?"

"I can't think of anything, I must look terrible."

"You do but I'm more concerned about how you feel. I want to get your fever down and that means we're going to pull off some of these blankets." She pulled back the blankets and noticed he was soaked through. "We need some dry clothes. Mr. Larson is probably going to need some too. I'll put that on the list." She sponged Denley down again and excused herself to check on Mr. Larson's condition.

Rosie had already changed the water and rags and Ashley sponged him down and pulled back some of the blankets. He was much weaker than Denley but he also had been sick a little longer. "Rosie if you can keep Mr. Larson sponged down like I'm doing then I'll tend to Mr. Denley. I want you to wash with lots of soap often to keep it contained. And keep changing the water and rags." Ashley looked around the room and noticed a carpet bag on a chair in the corner. Going through it she found a change of clothes and asked Rosie to get a couple of clean sheets. "We're going to change Mr. Larson's clothes and the sheet under him at the same time."

Rosie went for the sheets and while she did that Ashley went and washed her hands with soap and went back in to check on Denley and sponge him down before they started on Mr. Larson.

Washing their hands again they went back into Mr. Larson's room and began the task. It was not an easy thing to do because of how weak Mr. Larson was but Rosie was a robust woman with a lot of strength and Ashley was thankful for that. When they were working on getting his trousers off they noticed some terrible scarring on his right leg from the middle of his thigh down to almost the ankle.

Ashley winced as she looked at it, "Oh that had to hurt."

Rosie was looking at it and making a face, "That explains why he always limps so badly. My, that has to hurt terrible even still." They finished getting him dressed and the sheets back in place.

"Have you known him long Rosie?"

"I have. He comes ever so often but not so big for talk." Rosie took the rag from Ashley, "Aye love, I can do that. You best go check on Dr. Denley now."

Ashley returned to Denley's room and began sponging him down again. He wanted to talk but was weak and Ashley didn't want him using the energy. "Shsh I'm back. Don't tire yourself." She heard a knock on the front door and rushed out. It would be Dr. Kerrington coming for the list.

"What's the situation like in there? How is Denley?"

"He's burning up. I've sponged him down a few times now and peeled back some of the blankets but he needs a change of clothes. He's soaked right through and I want to get him into something dry. Mr. Larson had some clothes here so we were able to change him. I also need some things brought from the clinic." She rattled off the list. "Did you talk to Elizabeth?"

"Yes I talked to her, she thinks Margaret Golde might be able to help and she's been exposed to the fever too; but if she has to help out she can't return to the house. She doesn't want Katie exposed so Maggie will look after her if that happens. Other than that she said to just take care of Denley and help him get better. I've brought some of the things on your list; I'll leave them at the door. I'll go get the change of clothes and the rest of the things right away. It's a good idea to get him into clean dry sheets.

As Dr. Kerrington was climbing into his carriage Ashley opened the door and picked up the box of things he had brought. She placed it on a small table at the entrance and looked through it to see what was sent. There was a large bottle of alcohol, a smaller one of laudanum, and some sponges. There was also lots of soap for washing their hands. It was obvious Elizabeth had added to the box too. There was a change of clothes for Ashley and some sheets that Ashley recognized as well as some bread, butter and cheese and two jars of soup; one more like a stew for Rosie and herself and the other was just a clear broth for Denley and Mr. Larson.

They continued sponging the men down as they waited for Dr. Kerrington to return. The men were resting quietly when he finally did come back.

"I'll check back on you this evening. Don't tire yourselves out. If it gets to be too much I'll get someone to spell you off." He left the supplies at the door the way he had the first time and headed for the carriage.

Taking the supplies upstairs she called to Rosie. "We can change Denley's sheets and clothes now. Dr Kerrington has brought a change for him and it would be good to do it as soon as possible. When we get that finished there is some broth we can try and get into the men. Elizabeth has also sent a stew for us."

"I'll just sponge Mr. Larson down again before we start."

Ashley went into Denley again. She sponged him down one more time but there didn't seem to be much change. He was still burning up. He kept trying to talk but Ashley kept shushing him. Don't use your energy."

He wasn't going to be shushed though, "How did you find me? I need to know why you came. Is Katie ok, I didn't give this to her did I?"

"Katie is fine. I had gone to the clinic to see how you were doing. We are still family; I needed to know you were ok. When Dr. Kerrington said he hadn't seen you in days and had no clue were you were, he told me someone came in the evening and that you took your medical bag and left. I just remembered something Rosie told me. Remember when you brought me here so I could talk to her about William? Well she said that you would come here sometimes when she had someone come in here that needed medical attention. It was the only place I could think of to look. Now I've answered your question so please rest.' She put the rag back into the bowl of water and wiped her hands dry. "Now when Rosie comes in, we're going to change your sheets and clothes and get some broth into you. It's best to get you into something dry."

It wasn't the answer he had hoped for. He had hoped she had changed her mind about what she told him, "Just leave me be."

"We'll be discreet. You don't have to worry about that but we need you in dry clothes."

"I'm not worried about you being discreet. You shouldn't have come." He was really straining to talk and it took most of his energy. He relaxed against the pillow unable to fight her. She had her mind made up and nothing was going to change it.

Rosie washed her hands when she came in and they propped Denley up and stripped the sheet off the top end of the bed. With Denley leaning against Ashley, Rosie quickly fit the sheet over the top of the bed and tucked it in. Ashley unbuttoned Denley's shirt and stripped it off while Rosie quickly sponged his back down and wiped him dry. They had a dry shirt on him and he was laid back down against his pillow. Now they had to pull the damp sheet off completely from under his legs and pull the dry one into place which Rosie did quite efficiently. Then draping a sheet over Denley's lower body they discreetly removed his pants and put on the dry ones. They worked quickly so he wouldn't catch a chill. They wanted him to cool down with the fever but they didn't want pneumonia to be a problem.

Rosie went in to check on Mr. Larson and sponge him down again. "You're a good person to be caring for me so. If I don't make it I want to thank you. I need you to know that."

It was Rosie's turn to shush him. "Aye, you'll make it alright, and I don't want to hear you talk like that no more."

Ashley was just outside the door and heard the conversation. Could Rosie be a bit sweet on him? He was about her age or maybe a little older. He wasn't what you would call handsome but he wasn't ugly either. He had a thick crop of dark curly hair and looked to be a bit rugged; maybe a dock worker at one time. He looked to be a bit short and stocky with a crooked nose.

When Rosie came out she quickly wiped her eyes and washed her hands acting as if nothing had been said. They went into the kitchen to dish out some of the broth. It was a small room but it was serviceable and good enough for one person. There was a small porch off the kitchen with a door leading to a small back yard. There were a few chickens running around the yard and a burning barrel in one corner. That would come in handy for disposing of Mr. Larson and Denley's clothes and some of the rags that have been over used.

Ashley was lost in thought as she looked around. All she could think of was how terrible Denley was. The fever was so bad and she was hoping it would start to drop, but of course she had only arrived today. Perhaps tomorrow he will show improvement.

"The broth is ready to go. We should go and see if we can get this into them." Rosie's words brought Ashley back to the present.

They carried the bowls up the stairs and headed for different rooms. Ashley sponged Denley's face down first and propped his head up a bit. He looked so different with his unshaven face. She brought a spoon of broth to his mouth and coaxed him to eat. "It will do you some good to get something into you. Elizabeth had it sent with Dr. Kerrington."

"I don't feel like eating. Why not go help Rosie with Mr. Larson. How is he doing?"

"He hasn't changed and Rosie doesn't need my help. I'm not leaving this room so you may as well eat a bit." Indicating that she was still holding the spoon and not giving in he allowed her to feed him a small amount. She sponged his face and neck down again and moved a lock of hair away from his eyes to do his forehead.

To him even as sick as he was it felt like a caress. It was so emotionally distressing to have her here looking after him. As badly as he wanted her not to leave his side he knew the longer she was beside him the harder it would be later. "I have a terrible head ache, can you please leave and let me sleep now."

"I'll get you some Laudanum." She left the room and decided to see how Mr. Larson was doing. Rosie was still feeding him and he seemed to be responding better than Denley but has also been sick for a few extra days. It was at least a good indication that a recovery was possible. She returned to Denley's room with a dose of Laudanum and took his bowl to the kitchen. She sat and waited for Rosie to come down and then they could have something to eat. It was going to be a long night.

Long night was an understatement. Denley's head ache worsened and his body ached, his fever seemed to go up and Ashley spent hours wiping him down. He was too sick to care and he didn't have the strength to fight Ashley. Rosie assured her that Mr. Larson had been every bit as sick as Denley and was making some progress.

Mr. Larson slept through the night and Rosie checked on him every hour but he didn't need anything so she helped spell Ashley off from time to time, though Ashley didn't like leaving the room for too long at a time in case there were any changes.

By morning you could tell Mr. Larson would make a complete recovery even though he was weak he had no fever and the body aches were easing up. He even had more energy in his voice. He asked Rosie if she would mind helping him with a shave and by noon he was wanting a little more than broth to eat.

Denley on the other hand was not doing as well. He wasn't trying to help himself either. Ashley had to fight to get any broth into him and he kept trying to get her to leave the room. Finally in a moment of sheer frustration she threw the rag into the bowl,

"If you want to give up then fine but I don't have to watch it! I'll send for Margaret Golde to tend to you. I'll send a letter to your mother telling her how you gave up. Don't worry about Katie, she'll miss you but she is young enough to forget about you and as for me well, I thought I could live with out you in my life but I never imagined it this way. I had expected you to find a nice young woman to marry and give you a house full of children. I could stand that, but to sit and watch you die; I would rather die myself." She stormed out of the room with him too weak to say anything and he watched her through eyes glassy from the fever.

Rosie was the one that came in the next couple of times to cool him down and tend to him. He summoned the strength to ask where Ashley was and Rosie replied, "She told me she had an important letter to write and wants it done before Dr. Kerrington comes back to check on things."

"Please get her for me."

Rosie left the room and Ashley came in. "What do you want? I have things to take care of before Dr. Kerrington comes which should be very soon."

"I want you. I don't want Margaret Golde, and I don't want a letter sent to mother. I won't give up." That was all the energy he had.

He was true to his word, he took his broth when she fed him, the Laudanum when he needed it for the pain and she sponged him down regularly. By the next day he was showing improvement.

Mr. Larson was sitting up for his meals and feeding himself. He and Rosie spent a lot of time together with Rosie doing most of the talking.

"I've got me nerve up and I want to know Rosie if you would consider becoming me wife. I wanted to ask you months ago but I couldn't find the words for it. I don't have anything to offer except me self. If you need time to think it over that's fine. If the answer might be yes then you have to see me leg cause it's an ugly mess and you have to be able to stand the sight of it. If the answer is no then I'll understand and I'll not hold it against you."

"I've seen your leg when we had to change your clothes. You told me you were in an accident and that's why you limp, does it still hurt?"

"Aye it does hurt. I worked in a shipyard and a steel beam was being lifted and it slipped and landed on me and three other men. I was the only one that lived but it destroyed me leg. Does that mean you're thinking on it?" he asked with a hopeful smile on his face.

"Aye I'll think on it. Mind I'm only thinking on it, I haven't said yes.

It took a number of days until Denley was well enough to be taken home but with the fever gone it was just a matter of building his strength back up after being down for so long. Ashley was determined to have him taken to her home where he could be cared for properly. Dr. Kerrington volunteered to stay on as long as necessary.

11
Planning a Future

Denley and Ashley were invited to attend a very private wedding ceremony for Mr. Larson and Rosie and they would hold off until Denley was well enough to attend. Denley kept his heart guarded but was waiting until the time was right before he asked Ashley about something she had said to him when he had given up. It was what gave him a reason to fight. He was sitting propped up with pillows when Ashley entered the room and now was a good time. As far as he could discern Elizabeth had gone to town to purchase a wedding gift and had taken Katie with her, and Maggie and Ellen were upstairs.

"You said at Rosie's that you could live without me but you expected me to…how did you put that-find a nice young woman to marry and give me a house full of children. That's what it's all about isn't it. It didn't have anything to do with you not being over William."

"Denley I don't want to go over this again." She stood to leave the room but he grabbed her by the wrist.

"But I do. I need to. If it's about you not being able to give me a house full of children shouldn't that be something we both discuss together? If that's the reason you don't want to be with me then we should discuss it. Don't hide behind William for an excuse."

"Ok. That's it, that's the real reason. The day before we came home from Newcastle mother Pauline told me you would be a wonderful father and she couldn't wait for all the little grandchildren that would be running around her house when we go for holidays. I know you would make a wonderful father too. I see you with Katie and I just couldn't bear it if you started to resent me later because I couldn't give you children of your own."

"Ashley, I've thought about that too, but it's a loss for both of us. I was there to deliver Katie and I know what I had to tell you when you were strong enough to handle the thought of never having children. I also told you I hoped I was wrong. But whether I was right or wrong it doesn't change the way I feel about you or Katie. You can make decisions for yourself but you can't make decisions for me. I will never resent you and I can be a good uncle/father for Katie. You don't have to go through this alone. Let me be with you." He paused and then finished, "Oh, one more thing; don't wait around for me to find a nice young lady, because I already found her and no one else can or will ever take her place." He released the hold he had on her wrist, "Please think about what I've said and we can talk about it after the wedding" he pleaded.

She nodded and left the room unable to say anything. What could she say? He was right. She let the real reason slip when Denley had given up the will to live. She hadn't thought he would even remember that conversation but she would have said whatever it took to make him accept her help or at least someone's help. Her thoughts were interrupted when Elizabeth arrived back from her shopping. Denley made an appearance in the doorway, being his fist time out of bed without assistance he was weak but able to steady himself.

"What are you doing up without help?" Elizabeth scolded, "You should be asking for help until you build your strength back up."

"I have to start getting up and around. We have a wedding to attend in a couple of days and I need to be able to stand on my own by then. I was thinking it is time to have a shave and was wondering if a bowl of water could be brought in and I could have a bit of help, I'm not sure if my hand will be steady enough.

Elizabeth quickly glanced at Ashley, not sure of the situation between the two of them and ready to offer if Ashley didn't. She hadn't helped a man shave since her husband's death. She was relieved when Ashley quickly offered to bring the bowl and towels in. His shaving equipment had been brought from his house days ago when Ashley and Elizabeth had gone for a change of clothes for him.

Wrapping a towel around his neck she tucked it in and lathered his face, then, she had to be honest with him. "I only ever watched William do this. I never actually helped him."

"You'll do fine. I'm more worried if I attempt it to only get it half done or slipping and cutting myself. You at least have a steady hand and I can talk you through it."

So with the blade in her hand he told her what angle to hold it and what direction to go and within a few minutes he was looking like the Denley she was familiar with. She double checked and then gently wiped the remaining lather off his face. She carefully wiped the blade off and cleaned and put away everything. She moved the big water bowl to a table by the door and sat back down by his bed. "You tricked me. You're so sneaky; you knew I would volunteer to spare Elizabeth from having to do that."

"It worked too."

"Yes. I was wondering if we could have that talk now instead of waiting until after the wedding. I don't need time to think about it. I had the whole time you were sick to think about it."

"Ok but promise me you'll be honest with me and with yourself. You don't need to protect me or decide how you think I will feel about having or not having children."

"That's fair. I owe you an apology. It was wrong for me to use William as an excuse. I didn't want you to know the real reason because I knew you would try and change my mind; but I'm scared. Not of living with you; but without you. When you were sick and pushing me away it hurt and I realized how much I hurt you when I pushed you away. I never imagined you would be willing to give up on life though."

"So we can put this behind us. We enjoy the good times and hold each other up through the tough times. I have one more request; will you please wear that rose colored dress to the wedding."

"Consider it done." She moved closer to him, "Do you remember that kiss in the garden?"

"I do and this seems like a good time to finish that; come here…" and he wrapped his arms around her in a way that felt like he would never let her go.

The wedding of Rosie Boyle and Nick Larson was attended by Denley, Ashley, Elizabeth, and Dr. John Kerrington. It was a nice ceremony and they all went back to Elizabeth's for tea and cakes. Ashley prohibited Denley from drinking anything stronger than tea because he was still not 100 percent recovered. Denley managed to get Elizabeth off to the side un-noticed and asked if she would mind watching Katie for the evening. He wanted to take Ashley out for dinner seeing she was all dressed up.

They enjoyed a nice afternoon and by 3:00 Nick and Rosie were headed back to the boarding house. Nick was going to help

Rosie run the business and help keep up the maintenance. It had some things needing attention that had been long overdue. He felt he owed Rosie a great deal. He found her shortly after he recovered from the accident at the shipyard and that gave him reason to return, and she looked after him during the fever. He could never do for her what she did for him.

As they were watching Nick and Rosie leave in their carriage Ashley noticed Denley's carriage ready to go. "It looks like you're planning to return to your house now."

"Not tonight. I am going to pack up my things and return home tomorrow though. It's time and I think I can care for myself now. Did I ever thank you for pushing me to get better?"

"Yes; too many times to count," she said with a big smile.

"Well just add one more time. Go get your wrap because we have reservations for dinner and Elizabeth will care for Katie."

"Isn't it a little early?" she asked as he followed her back into the house.

"Yes but we can take a ride through the park first."

Ashley went in and adjusted her hat on her head, pulled on a pair of gloves and wrapped her shawl around her shoulders. She gave Katie a kiss and was led out the door and helped into the waiting carriage.

Denley climbed up and took his seat beside her. Everything was right again and he was going to make sure it stayed that way. He had made arrangements for Mr. Whitfield to drive the carriage and directed him toward the park. He found a quiet little spot near a stream and had Mr. Whitfield pull the horses to a halt.

"What are you up to?"

"Well you were right, it is too early for dinner so how about a short stroll. The air is fresh and I need the walking. It helps me build up my strength. But we won't go too far. You would look funny trying to carry me back," he teased. Taking her by the hand he led her past a little bench nestled in a cluster of roses and shrubs. There was some willow trees swaying in a slight breeze and farther down the path was a little stone bridge crossing over the trickling stream. He stopped her on the middle of the bridge and turned to face her. Still holding her by the hand he kneeled on one knee.

Ashley had instant butterflies waiting for what was to follow.

"Ashley Grey Radcliff you have touched my heart like no one ever has. Will you do me the honor of becoming my wife; will you marry me?"

Ashley didn't hesitate, her eyes sparkled. "Yes, Mr. Denley Radcliff I'll marry you. I know I can't live without you and I wouldn't want to."

Standing up he pulled a small pouch out of his pocket and tipped it into the palm of his hand to reveal a ring. "This was my grandmother's ring and my mother wore it and she passed it onto me when we were in Newcastle. I hope it fits." She slipped her glove off and held her hand out to him and he slipped it onto her finger. It was a band engraved to look like gold lace and had an antique colored diamond in the center.

Ashley held her hand out to admire it on her finger. "Oh Denley it's absolutely beautiful."

He wrapped one of his arms around her waist and put his other hand on the back of her head with his fingers entangled in her hair and kissed her gently at first. Light kisses on her forehead and down to her cheek. Then he made his way to her lips and kissed her with a passion that was very similar to the kiss in the garden only this time he didn't pull away. He didn't want the moment to end. He made his way down her neck and then back to her mouth again. When they finally drew apart he cupped her face with his hands and with the biggest smile told her she had just made him the happiest man ever.

"We better get back to the carriage. You said we have dinner reservations."

"Yes we do." Reluctantly he dropped his hands from her face. She smoothed her dress down and admired the ring on her finger again before he took her by the hand and began to lead her back to the carriage.

They sat in a secluded corner requested by Denley. "I know you made me promise no liquor today but I think a small glass of wine to celebrate would be fine; but I won't if it will upset you."

"A glass of wine would be a nice touch."

While eating their dinner they discussed the choices that they were faced with. "We have some things to figure out but I don't want to wait. I am a doctor that owns a shipyard; not to mention it happens to be in Newcastle but my practice is here and this is also yours and Katie's home. It doesn't matter where we live but we have to find a home big enough. My house is too small. It's designed for a single doctor and we have a family. Oh that sounds so good."

"Slow down a bit. It's a lot to take in, especially in a matter of a few hours. We are going to decide together, right?" She hadn't thought of the idea of moving to Newcastle; it's not that she didn't love Mother Pauline, but she really liked it here and the idea of leaving was overwhelming.

"Absolutely; I won't make any decisions without your agreement. "I am considering asking Dr. Kerrington to stay on but that won't affect our decisions. It will just lighten my load at the clinic and give me some time to deal with the shipyard and other holdings."

"Speaking of the shipyard, did Rosie tell you Mr. Larson used to work in a shipyard and was injured on the job?" She wanted to change the topic so she had time to consider things.

"No, I had been told about his leg being messed up and that's why he limps but how it happened never came up. Did he say which shipyard?"

"No, I should have asked but we were both distracted by very sick men. I'll visit Rosie in a few days and see if I can find out."

"I am played right out. Would you be disappointed if we left now?"

"No, of course you mustn't overdo things and this has been a very busy day. Are you sure you're ready to go back to your place yet?" She was worried he would push himself too hard.

"I'm sure I'll be fine, but right now I want to pay the bill and leave before I collapse."

Back at home they shared their news with Elizabeth then Denley excused himself to turn in. He would have liked to tell his mother first but the ring would have been impossible to hide. He gave Ashley a quick kiss on the cheek and left the room.

Elizabeth and Ashley sat up talking about the decisions her and Denley were now facing.

When morning arrived Ashley had to look at the ring on her finger to make sure it hadn't been a dream. It felt so strange, yet it was real. She heard Katie stirring in her room and went and tended to her. When both were washed and dressed she carried Katie down stairs and headed for the breakfast room. It was smaller than the dining room but cozier. It allowed for a good view of the garden which was at its peak for beauty this time of the year. It also allowed the morning sun to light up the room. She caught sight of Elizabeth out having her morning tea and decided to join her. Maggie and Ellen were always up early and busy with their tasks long before Ashley and Katie made it down. Elizabeth was less predictable but this morning she was up early as well. They sat and talked about the garden and sipped their tea as they waited for Denley.

"Maybe I should check on him. Yesterday tired him out considerably. I worry he might be going back to his home too soon if he leaves today."

"I'm sure he knows what he's doing. Let him sleep. We can have our breakfast now. I'm sure Katie is getting hungry."

Ellen was cleaning up their dishes before Denley finally appeared. He looked a little embarrassed that he had slept so late. "I wanted to be up early this morning, I have so much to do."

Katie rushed into his arms for a hug and then wanted down to chase after Snowball.

Ellen brought out breakfast for Denley, and Elizabeth excused herself, "I'm sure you two have a lot to talk about. I understand you have decided to return to your house today but please join us for dinner tonight. I am planning a special dinner to celebrate your engagement." Elizabeth's words caused Victoria [Ellen] to stop in her tracks.

She had obviously not noticed the ring or heard the news until just now. She glanced in Ashley's direction. "Congratulations." She smiled at both and headed back indoors with Elizabeth behind her wanting to go over the menu for the evening.

Finally alone to talk both started at the same time and Ashley stopped to allow Denley to talk. "In order to set a date we have to decide where we will make our home. It's a big decision but I really don't want a long engagement," then he added jokingly, "I don't want to give you time to change your mind."

"That, I can assure you is not going to happen. I have a question for you first. What will you be the happiest doing; tending the shipyard or being a doctor? I think that has to be decided first."

"I am hoping that if Dr. Kerrington accepts my offer I will be able to do both. If I do both then settling here makes sense. This is where you want to be, isn't it?"

"I do like it here and Elizabeth has made me like family but it has to work for both of us."

"If we settle here I can look after the shipyard from here as long as I can hire some one I trust to manage it, but it will mean I will have to be away at times if problems occur. Will it upset you if I have to travel?"

"No and Katie and I can travel with you at times. I'm sure Mother Pauline would like it if we came along."

"With my practice I need to be close to town. I can't change that. I don't think we need a house as big as what I grew up in, but maybe one this size will be big enough," he gestured toward the house. "Would that suite you?"

"Have you seen the size of this house inside; it's way too big for three people."

"We'll hire someone to do the cooking and cleaning. So we need to find a house and pick a date. Now I have to be on my way. I have to see Dr. Kerrington and see what he thinks about taking on part of the practice. I also need to get back to work or at least build back up to it. I will see you at dinner tonight." He gave her a light kiss on the cheek and left.

She sat wondering how soon he wanted to get married. His mother would obviously expect to be invited and would need the time to make arrangements. She also needed to send Josie a letter and tell her that she was now engaged. She was going to be very busy over the next while especially if she and Denley would be looking for a house. She spent an afternoon writing the letter and making a list of things she needed to do and things she hadn't discussed with Denley yet.

After the dinner that evening Denley gathered up his things still in the bedroom he used and left early. He had been busy and was quite tired. He had to admit he had overdone it and he would pay every time until he had fully recuperated. Going over the list of things they needed to discuss would have to wait until tomorrow.

When Ashley arrived at Rosie's the next day Mr. Larson was busy replacing some floor boards that had been rotting away. "He's bin bangin on boards on and off all day. How's your Dr. Denley doin?"

"Probably the same as yours but not banging on boards. He tried to go back to work today. He overdoes it and plays out early. I have news though. Look we're engaged!"

"Ah love, I'm so pleased for you. He's a good man, Denley is. You take care of him and he'll look after you good."

"Doesn't Mr. Larson's leg hurt doing that kind of work?" Ashley was fishing for a way to ask where he worked when that happened without being too obvious.

"You best call him Nick. That's what he wants. He asked me why you kept callin him 'Mr.' when you were here. He's not one for all that proper talk."

"I'll try and remember that. I don't remember if you ever told me where Mr…I mean Nick came from?"

"He's come from Newcastle, but he won't be goin back ever."

"Well I should hope not. He's married to a business woman now."

Rosie chuckled at the term business woman. She had never thought of herself that way.

"I have to be going, but I wanted to come by and give you our news before Denley beat me to it."

Nick quit hammering long enough to come over and say hello.

Rosie quickly burst in with the news of their engagement and Nick offered his congratulations.

"Thank-you Nick," Ashley made a point of using his first name.

"Ah Rosie spoke to ya about calling me 'Mr'.

"Yes she did, and I'm sorry if it made you uncomfortable. Anyhow, I was just telling Rosie I have to leave but I'll come by when I can stay a little longer and have a cup of tea with her."

After saying there good-byes Ashley headed to the clinic to tell Denley what she had found out. When she entered she was met by Dr. Kerrington.

"I'm expecting Denley back any minute if you want to wait."

She sat down and only had to wait a couple of minutes before Denley entered whistling a tune. "I was hoping you would come by today. We can talk privately in here," he opened a door and led her into an examining room.

"I just came back from Nick and Rosie's and she said he's from Newcastle, so if he was hurt at the shipyard; your ship yard why did he not have anything to offer but himself when he married Rosie. Did your father not pay off injured people in his employment?"

"I assumed he did but I will definitely have to look into it. I'll probably have to make a trip out to Newcastle and get his file to look at. Oh I just got back from looking at a house. I wanted to know if it was a good prospect before I show it to you. It's the house at the end of Willow Brook Road. It's the one with the big trees in the front. You probably know the one."

"I know it. It's been empty for almost a year but it's a huge house; way too big for just three of us."

"Well, yes it is a little bigger than what we were looking for but we don't have to fill all the rooms and I can turn one of the rooms on the main floor into an office. With a house that size we would have to hire some staff. It has a big kitchen and a nice garden in the back that you would enjoy. We don't have to buy this one but take a look at it before you decide."

"Ok, I'll look at it with you, but it is a very large house, though I do have to say I like the location. It's within walking distance to Elizabeth's. Are you going to be coming by this evening? We have a few more things to talk about and I would rather do it at home than here."

"I can if you like. When I finish up here I'll clean up and come by." He gave her a quick kiss before she opened the door to leave.

That evening they were able to discuss a few things and Denley offered to take her through the house the next day.

The horse trotted down the road and over the small wooden bridge. It had cedar shakes on the roof and the sides of it were painted red. The sound of the horse's hooves on the planks made a hollow sounding noise that Ashley felt she would never tire of hearing. It was a nice park like area that wound its way through the trees and then they turned right onto Willow Brook Road and through the gates down between the big trees on the property. The house sat nestled within some smaller trees farther back from the entrance and it looked so peaceful. There was a large entrance with a small room just off to one side for boots and coats in the winter and there was shelves for hats and gloves to keep them neat. Heading farther into the house through the sitting room there was a large dinning room and a smaller room that felt rather cozy. Ashley could feel herself liking this room the most and it had a door that led into the garden space that Denley told her about. It had been sadly neglected and would take some time to make it appeasing to the eyes.

The kitchen was large and had two stoves for preparing large meals and good sized counters for food preparation. Ashley had childhood dreams of doing her own cooking but now she actually had a hard time imagining cooking at all. When she was with William the cooking was done for them or they ate out. Some of her fondest memories with Josie were their attempts at cooking that always had them laughing uncontrollably. With a house this size staff would definitely need to be hired to maintain it.

Walking back to the dinning room there was a small room off it that Denley said would make a fine office, he would need some shelves put in and it needed a fresh coat of paint. The staircase handrail and spindles were made out of mahogany with a rich but nicely worn oil finish and spiraled up to the middle floor. There was a sitting room at the top of the stairs with a fire place to make it cozy. At the one end of the sitting room was a wide hall with four large bedrooms on one side and three smaller rooms on the other side. At the end of the hall was a door that led to a smaller staircase that led up to the maid's quarters and were designed to give them privacy when they were off duty but also led down to the kitchen as a short cut. There was a table on each side of the door that would have been a valuable help for the staff to place trays or water pitchers on to free their hands for opening the door. Denley seemed enthused as he revealed each room pointing out the best qualities. The sleeping chambers all had fireplaces in them and the largest room had a dressing room that was big enough to be a separate bed room but did not lead out into the hall. Most of the wood trim was dark tones making the rooms feel rich and warm. The pieces of furniture that had been left were covered with white sheets to protect them from dust but taking a peek under the sheets revealed beautiful rich woods and tapestry covered chairs. Ashley couldn't imagine anyone leaving such beautiful furniture behind. All the window coverings had been left and were very elegant. It was a house you couldn't help but fall in love with but to Ashley it seemed like the house should have a large family in it, not just the three of them.

"It is a lovely house but it is really large. I just have a hard time imagining living in such a big house," Ashley sighed, "but it looks to me like you have set your heart on it. It would need a good cleaning and some painting before anyone could possibly move in."

"I think this is the perfect house for us and I am positive you can make it a home. If you are comfortable with this I will make the arrangements. Did you notice the stables in the back?"

"No I guess I will have to go back and take a look at them. I was looking more to the garden area. It must be tucked off to the side more." She paused a moment and looking around she gave in, "I guess that is settled then. We now have a house but it needs cleaned and painted. We need to find out how long that will take and then we can set a date."

"We can set a date any time. I can make enough room in my place for you and Katie for a short while. I could store some of my belongings here once we have the keys. Why don't you come with me to Newcastle and we can pick out a few items to give it your own personal touch. I have to go and get the files on Nick Larson and find out what happened to him. It's going to be a quick trip and perhaps Elizabeth would be willing to watch Katie. If you want we can stop over in Sheffield and do some shopping there and you could have a chance to visit Josie."

"I would love to go but it's a lot to take in so fast. We haven't even left the house and you're already talking about furniture and a trip to Newcastle and setting a wedding date."

"That's because I don't want to wait a minute longer than I have to, to make you my wife.

"Well I'll make it easy for you. How about if we get married two weeks from Saturday; that will give us time to invite mother Pauline and Josie. I doubt Josie will be able to get away with three children but I should still invite her."

"So you're thinking of a honeymoon in Newcastle. Well you just made that decision so easy and I'm not going to complain with that one at all. I guess Newcastle can wait a couple of weeks if you don't mind me getting Nick Larson's file when we're on our honeymoon."

"We have a lot to do then and standing here is wasting time. We need to sign the papers for the house and get painters in it as quickly as possible."

Ashley was so excited when she was telling Elizabeth about the house. "I wonder what kind of history it has. It seems strange that a beautiful house like that would be empty for so long."

"It is a lovely house. They used to have grand parties in it. My husband and I used to go to them. They would hire an orchestra to play and there would be dancing and huge feasts. We would have a wonderful time. They had nine children and I only remember meeting three or four of them. The rest had married and moved away. Albert Fenwick was the owner at that time. His brother Stanley lived with them and after my husband died Mr. Fennwick, Stanley had his eye on me. I wasn't interested in getting married again so eventually he moved on and got married. But the rest of the Fennwick family just moved without a word. One of the children died in the house and it was said that Mrs. Fennwick couldn't bear to live there any more. It totally destroyed her. I have no idea where they went or if they are even together anymore. Some times the loss of a child can destroy any happiness you thought you had."

"So it does have some history; with you."

Elizabeth sighed. "Yes and probably more from other owners because I don't think Mr. Fenwick had that house built. It seems like a lifetime ago. I am happy for you. It will be nice to see the inside of the house again."

12
So Much to Do

Everything was set into motion. Denley signed the papers for the house and he hired a crew of painters followed by cleaners to wash walls and floors. There was so much to get done and time was running out. Why did she suggest getting married in two weeks; she should have given them more time. The telegrams were sent out so there was no going back. The days started to go by fast after that.

"I think you have over looked something very important. Have you decided what to wear for your wedding?" Elizabeth asked. "We need to go shopping; tomorrow. You need a dress and so does Katie. I think Katie's will be easy to find but we need to make a trip to Oxford for yours. I think you would look good in cream or ecru."

"Oh I can't believe I've been so busy with painters I didn't even think of my dress. Of coarse we need to go shopping."

"I'm glad you thought of that. Everything else seems to be going well."

"Have you given any idea to hiring staff?"

"No that is on the list of things to do when we return. Denley is over at the house today with Mr. Larson. He hired him to oversee the changes needed to turn the one bedroom into an office. The kitchen will be ready in a couple of days and then I will have to stock it with some non perishable staples. I was hoping I could have your cook Mrs. Whitfield come with me and take a look at the kitchen and see if she can help me arrange it properly?"

"That won't be a problem; in fact I think she would probably enjoy the opportunity and the chance to see the inside of your house. You have a lot of things to do still. Do you think you'll have everything ready in time?"

"No, I'm going over to the house now to talk to talk to Denley about that. When I suggested two weeks I had no idea what I was expecting to have accomplished but it is not working out quite the way I planned. Mrs. Whitfield can walk over when she's able. I like it that we will be living so close. I look forward to our shopping trip tomorrow." She finished the last of her tea and left with Katie for the short walk.

Denley was looking out the window and watched them walking up the cobble stone path. They were going to be married in nine days and he could hardly wait. He met them out on the walk way and scooped Katie up and led Ashley around to the back garden. When they were out of sight of the painters he put Katie down so she could put both his arm around Ashley. "It seems like I haven't seen you in days. I've been so busy with all the painters and Nick with the office. Do you know it's only nine days before we're married?"

"I know; and I don't think we'll get everything ready in time."

"Well, I did say we could move into my place for a short time if we need to and I think we will probably have to do that. Things seem to be going slower than I had hoped.

"Well let's plan that and I don't have to panic about everything else. I'm waiting for Elizabeth's cook, Mrs. Whitfield. She's going to look through the kitchen with me to help me make a list of things we need for the kitchen. I should get inside in case she is here already."

"I'll keep Katie with me if you want. We can do some exploring until you're finished. Ashley there is something we have never talked about and I think we should." She turned to look at him trying to think of anything she had missed and he continued, "What do you want Katie to call me? I don't know if you want her to call me uncle or 'father,' I mean once we're married."

"That's a hard one. You are her uncle but you are also the only man that has been in her life and you will be filling the role of father. If you want her to call you father that would be fine but I do want her to know as she's growing up that her true father was your brother William. Is that alright for you?"

"That will be perfect." He held out his hand to Katie and they walked toward the stables.

She gave Mrs. Whitfield a tour of the house and finished it in the kitchen where she was able to give Ashley some good ideas and tips on arranging things. When they were finished Ashley found Denley and Katie. Katie was due for her nap and Ashley wanted to get back and put some things together for her and Elizabeth's trip to Oxford. "I'll be gone for a good part of tomorrow. Elizabeth and I are going to Oxford to shop for my wedding dress. Will we see you this evening?"

"There is a very good possibility. Before I head back to the clinic I should see how Nick is doing. That's the one room I would like finished so I can store some of my things in it to make room for you and Katie." he gave her a hug and a kiss and they both headed in different directions.

Nick was sitting on a chair that had been left behind by the previous owners and he was looking some what troubled. As Denley approached he stood and confronted Denley, "I may not be schooled like you, and I can't read or write but I have me smarts about me. I just found out that you're a Radcliff from Newcastle. That means your family owns the shipyard that I got hurt in. I can't believe you been hiding that from me.

"Nick I don't know what to say except I was planning on getting your file when I go to Newcastle. I was returning from Newcastle when I treated you on the train. My father had just died and I actually am the new owner of the shipyard. I just found out that that is where your leg was injured."

"Aye, that's where it happened alright. Your Mr. Sherman said the accident was my fault and I cost them a great amount of money and was responsible for the death of three men. After meeting with him a few times once I was walking again he said if I was a smart man I would leave quickly and quietly. It happened last fall and I don't want no trouble."

"Do you remember exactly what happened?" Denley needed to know what Nick recalled if he was going to look into it.

"I remember like it was yesterday. It took four of us to secure the chains and hooks onto the ends of a steel beam, two on each end. When we had both ends secured I gave a thumbs up to the men working the hoist. They started lift'n it and when it got up so far it began to slip and we just couldn't get out of the way quick enough. It swung out of control taking part of the structure down with it and…well you can figure the rest."

"Nick I am so sorry that happened. I'm going to ask you not to say anything to anyone about this until I get back from Newcastle. I promise I am looking into what happened and why you didn't get paid some sort of compensation."

Denley headed back to the clinic after his discussion with Nick and pulled out the papers he had brought back from Newcastle and tucked them into a bag. Maybe a fresh pair of eyes would help him find what he was looking for. After he did a couple of house calls he was going to head over to see Ashley and show her the papers. Maybe she would see what he couldn't.

Dr. Kerrington came out of an examining room following a mother with a small child suffering from an ear infection. He was beginning to look quite comfortable in the office since he had accepted Denley's offer. It was working nicely for Denley as well. He was seeing to his patients in the afternoons allowing him to start as early in the morning as he wanted to on anything else which seemed to involve packing up some of his personal belongings. He was also spending some considerable time at the house on Willow Brook Road.

Visiting Ashley that evening he related to her the whole conversation he had with Nick and then pulled the papers out to show her and see if she could see anything odd about them.

"May I keep these for a couple of days to go over? I would like to look them over when there are no distractions and tonight you're distracting me."

"I can't have you distracted, maybe I should go," he teased. "You can pour over them for a few days. I'm going to be busy moving some of my things into the office at the house and getting my place ready for us."

"Did I tell you Elizabeth and I are going shopping tomorrow? We're looking for my wedding dress and something for Katie."

"Yes you mentioned that earlier today."

Ashley put Katie to bed for the night and they sat out on the porch talking over plans for the wedding. Elizabeth has already given permission for them to have their wedding in the garden. It was going to be small. Ashley hadn't really gotten to know too many people in the area and she didn't want Maggie and ~~Victoria~~ *Ellen* to have too much extra work.

Elizabeth and Ashley's trip to Oxford was a nice outing. They left Maggie in charge of Katie for the day so they didn't have to worry about her needs and could do as they pleased. They found a dress for Katie almost immediately. The top had short puff sleeves and embroidery on the front with buttons down the back. The skirt was done in layers of chocolate colored satin and lace alternating with bloomers to match. It also had little matching draw string purse.

They found a lady's shop and started looking for Ashley's dress. They found a couple of dresses in a rich cream color to try on. The first one had a plain top but the skirt was done in layers of silk lace. The second one was almost opposite. It had a very beautiful top with small glass beads and lace decorating the front which continued as a narrow panel all the way down the front to the floor and the rest of the skirt gathered tightly at the waist and flowed softly behind with a long train. Both dresses had at least fifty buttons down the back.

It was a hard decision to make as Katie's dress looked like it was made to go with the first dress but the second one fit better needing less alterations. It was Elizabeth that helped with the decision. She liked the beading on the second dress and with only a week left for the planning less alterations seemed to make the most sense. After having the dress picked out they could look at veils and shoes.

Ashley chased Elizabeth across the street to a tea house so she could pick out her silk stockings and garter and her corset before joining her when she was finished. They were thankful for having Mr. Whitfield bring them in the carriage instead of taking the coach.

The parcels were getting heavy and they still wanted to do more shopping. Elizabeth decided on a dress she had been eyeing up and went back to try it on. It was a deep royal blue taffeta with a small amount of lace on the top but was very elegant and it suited her coloring perfectly.

By the time they had finished all their shopping and were headed back to Harwell they were satisfied but tired.

Denley's day was very busy and exhausting as well. After having the desk and chair from his house put into the office at the new place he began moving some of his belongings and stacking them in the corner out of the way. By the time he was finished he had cleared enough space to make room for Ashley and Katie. It would be a bit cramped but it would be a good incentive to finish the work as quickly as possible so they could move in.

It was 2:00 in the morning when there was a pounding on the door. Maggie rose to answer it and lit a lantern so she could make her way down stairs and see who was at the door. Denley was standing there holding a small crying child about a year old. It was easy to see she was from the east side with the rags she was wearing. "Maggie I'm sorry to wake you but can you please go get Ashley for me."

She opened the door for Denley to step inside. "Of coarse, I'll be right back." When she woke Ashley, Elizabeth heard and she came out too."

"Maggie can you please take her, I'm sure Elizabeth will be fine with it but she needs a wash and a place to sleep. I need to talk to Elizabeth and Ashley and I'll wait here for them." She took the small child and Denley quickly added, "Her name is Hannah."

Elizabeth and Ashley met him at the entrance and Elizabeth escorted them into the study and closed the door. "I apologize for the hour and disturbing your sleep but this was my best option. Maggie has taken a small girl about a year old to clean up and put somewhere to sleep for the night. Her mother has just died from blood poisoning. The neighbor sent for me when she heard the child crying for so long without being tended to because it seemed so out of character for her. By the time I arrived she was almost dead and I could do nothing for her. The neighbor refused to take her as she has five of her own she has trouble feeding and her father is out to sea as far as she knows but she couldn't remember ever hearing his name. It appears we have an orphan on our hands. It's late and I hope you don't mind but we can deal with everything tomorrow. Her name is Hannah."

"No, of course you should have brought her here. We'll see that she is tended to and like you said we can deal with everything in the morning." Elizabeth then excused herself, "I'll just see that Maggie has found a place for Hannah and see that she is settled."

"I'll come by first thing in the morning. She's going to be a frightened little girl." He gave Ashley a lingering kiss and then left.

Ashley took a peek in Maggie's room. "I think she should be in the room with me Miss. If she wakes up she will be less frightened with someone here rather than in a strange house alone. I hope you don't mind but I found a night gown of Katie's for her."

"That's fine. We'll talk in the morning," she whispered back.

Hannah woke up frightened and crying. She was a tiny girl with big brown eyes and soft fine brown wispy hair. She was in need of a bath so Maggie had her all cleaned up and went through Katie's clothes to find something that she had grown out of.

Katie was excited to see a little girl. It was someone to play with.

Ashley's heart melted when she looked into her big scared eyes. Maggie handed her over to Ashley and left the room with other things to do. With only two days to the wedding there was still a lot of work needing attention and she didn't want Victoria left with it all.

Denley didn't make it over until just before 11:00. "I haven't been able to find out anything about her father and there is nothing in the mother's house to give any clues as to what ship he works on. None of her neighbors seem to know anything either. I'll have to contact the orphanage in Oxford and see if they have room for her."

"You can't possibly send her to an orphanage. Can't we look after her until we find some family?"

"Ashley, we have no idea if there is any family left and we don't know where to begin looking. If Hannah's father does return and finds Hannah and her mother gone he could return to sea without ever finding her. How long are you willing to look after her?" Denley was trying to be reasonable.

"I don't know. But look at her; she's scared. Everything she has known and been familiar with is gone. When I was attacked the one thing that comforted me was the knowledge that Katie would be looked after. Elizabeth would have fought for her if I would have died. I think we should do the same for Hannah even though we don't know much of anything about her."

"Are you forgetting we are to be married in two days and going to Newcastle for our honeymoon. Add that to the fact that when we return we will be cramped in my small place until the house is finished?"

Ashley put her hands out to take Denley's, "I'm sure we can manage, if we have too. I really want to do this. Once we're in our big place it will be one more room we can fill even if it is just temporary."

Elizabeth had just walked into the room in the middle of the conversation and caught the last little bit of what was said. "I'm sorry I didn't mean to walk in on a private conversation but I did over hear a bit. Turning to Denley she asked, "Do you need to send Hannah to the orphanage or is she able to be cared for by us?

"I don't need to send her there and it's the last place I would want to send any child. I could let them know we have her in case her father went there looking for her. But the timing is so bad."

"Well small children don't get to pick what happens." Then turning to Ashley she asked her, "Are you going to be able to give her up if her father is found even if it takes a year?"

"If I have too; I just feel like right now we would be doing the right thing for her."

"So both of you agree she would be better with us than in an orphanage and I agree too. Just wait here a moment," and Elizabeth left the room. When she returned she had Maggie with her. "What are your thoughts on sending Hannah to an orphanage? You were raised in one and would have the best advice."

"An orphanage is necessary for children with no place to go. But can't we keep her, I mean until her father or other family is found?"

"Are you willing to tend to her while Denley and Ashley are away?"

"I can do that. She won't be any trouble. Katie will help keep Hannah occupied too." Denley and Ashley sat quietly listening to the conversation between Elizabeth and Maggie.

"Well it appears to be settled then. I have to agree with the decision to keep Hannah for now as well"

Mother Pauline arrived Wednesday with three days left before the wedding and surprised Denley at the clinic. Mother Pauline always dressed so elegantly. She was almost overdressed for Harwell. Her hair always up and pinned with fancy hair pins that glittered when the light caught them a certain way. She was wearing a very deep blue gown that was trimmed with lace and she had it bustled at the back to keep it from dusting the ground. It had embroidery down the front with small pearl beads worked into it. Her jewelry looked like it was made to match.

They had much to talk about. She had no idea of the turmoil Denley had gone through when Ashley arrived home from

Newcastle or the fever that he had almost lost his life to. The most important thing he had to caution his mother on though, was to avoid any conversation leading to Ashley having children because that was not too likely to happen. She was disappointed to think that Katie would be her only grandchild but it was Denley's happiness that mattered to her and he knew this before he had ever grown any attachment to her.

The kitchen was a buzz with activity. The baking was being done and the smells of the pastries and cakes filled the house. The house was being given extra attention and big vases of cut flowers were placed around. The garden was being pruned and readied for the ceremony and Ashley was packing some of her trousseau for the trip to Newcastle and other things to be taken to Denley's when they returned.

Maggie knocked on the bedroom door, "Ashley, Mr. Radcliff has brought his mother over to see you. Shall I tell them you will be down shortly?"

"Yes thank-you Maggie. I'll just quickly freshen up and join them in the garden. Have tea brought out as well please."

Hannah shyly followed Katie around as she entertained her grandmother until Ashley was able to join them. They enjoyed their tea and some freshly baked scones and butter while catching up with all the latest news since they had last seen each other. Mother Pauline was being a little guarded about what subjects she pursued and which subjects she avoided. After a couple of hours of visiting Mother Pauline began to complain of a headache so before leaving Denley had promised that he and Ashley would give her a tour of the house on Willow Brook Road tomorrow after lunch.

On Thursday Elizabeth went to town to do a bit of shopping and take care of some personal business. Denley was going over some plans with Ashley when Elizabeth walked in and interrupted their conversation. She appeared to be a little on the pale side and Denley immediately noticed she didn't look well.

"Are you feeling alright Elizabeth? You look a little pale." Denley's doctoring skills were immediately noticed.

"I'm fine, but you best sit down. I'm afraid I have something to tell you that is not so easy to say. It appears you both have a very big problem to deal with. I was at my solicitors this morning to tend to some business and in our talking I was informed of a law that makes it illegal for you marry each other."

Both of them paled instantly and then Denley trying to recover asked, "What are you saying exactly?"

"There is a law that states a man cannot marry his brother's widow which is what Ashley is to you. I don't know how far reaching that law is. Perhaps you can go to a different country but that is something you should look into immediately. I'm going to excuse myself as you both have some very important things to discuss. I'm sorry to have been the one to tell you that news but I guess it's better to find this out today than the day of the wedding."

They sat starring at each other not sure what to say. What could they possibly do? Finally Denley spoke up. "I fell in love with you as Ashley Grey. I never gave it a thought that there could be such a law. I am going to see the solicitor and see if there are any exceptions or if there is any way around this. You'll go to a different country with me if that is the only way, won't you? Please tell me you will. I love you too much to live without you."

"Denley, what if there is no way around it?" she said as tears began to stream down her face.

"No. Don't think that way. I won't accept that for an answer. There just has to be something we can do." Getting to his feet he added, "As soon as I see the solicitor I'll let you know what I find out."

Denley left and then Elizabeth went in to see if Ashley was ok. "I called for some tea and you and I can wait together until Denley returns."

Ashley told Elizabeth about the idea of going to another country if that was possible but she was so distraught she didn't want to think about it. "What if we have to cancel the wedding? I don't want to lose Denley. I love him too much to let him go. What will we do? Oh, what will we do?" The tears began to fall and she covered her face with her hands to hide the emotion she was unable to contain.

This is one of those times Denley wished he knew how to ride a horse. It would have been quicker than taking the carriage. He snapped the reigns and started down the drive and passed John Kerrington with Pauline Radcliff by his side. John pulled up on the reigns but Denley continued on in a hurry.

When Pauline entered the house she found Ashley in such a terrible state. She began to express her disapproval of the way Denley passed without even stopping for a greeting and Elizabeth quickly gave her a look that stopped her from continuing. She sat quietly until Ashley had calmed a bit and it was only then that Elizabeth was willing to tell Pauline what had taken place.

Pauline started looking a little pale and within an hour she was complaining of a headache. Everyone sat quietly not really feeling like visiting while waiting for Denley to return.

Ellen brought in a tray of assorted pastries and a fresh pot of tea but they were hardly touched and Maggie kept the children entertained up in the nursery until it was time for their naps.

Denley waited impatiently until the solicitor had time to see him. He introduced himself as Harold Fines and extended a hand.

Denley got to the point immediately and what Elizabeth had told him was reinforced. There seemed to be no way around it at least locally and Mr. Fines could only offer to look into it further in other areas. It was going to take some time before he would be able to get back to Denley.

Denley arrived back at Elizabeth's quite distressed and led Ashley into the study to talk to her privately first. Sitting beside her he took both of her hands in his and giving them a reassuring squeeze he explained the situation. "I'm so sorry, but we are going to have to postpone the wedding. I refuse to believe there is no way around this. It's just going to take time to find out how we can get married legally." He pulled her into his arms and held her for the longest time. Finally he told her he should go and tell everyone what was happening. They would all be waiting anxiously.

Denley's mother wasn't feeling well and wanted to be taken back to her room immediately and Mr. Whitfield was asked to take her as Denley did not want to leave Ashley's side for the time being.

By Monday Mother Pauline was still not feeling well and decided to go back home to Newcastle. Denley could tell something was pressing on her mind but she had been unwilling to talk about it before she left. She told him it was just because she couldn't stand to see the disappointment in his eyes.

Denley visited every day to try and reassure Ashley but the time seemed to drag by so slowly waiting for the solicitor to find out anything helpful.

"I'm planning to go to Sheffield to get away from all of this turmoil. I need to clear my head and I can't do it here where everything reminds me of what we should already have had. We have a house we can't move into, this house was prepared, the baking done and my wedding dress hanging in my room."

"You'll be back though; you're not leaving me entirely are you?"

"No I want to see if Maggie will watch the children. For some obvious reasons I can't take Hannah and Katie wouldn't want to leave her behind. I'm only going to go for a few days, definitely no more than a week. You can go to Newcastle with Nick and get that settled with him. At least we won't be sitting around watching the clock and waiting for word from Mr. Fines."

"Can't we talk about this more? I'm so worried I will lose you."

"I've made up my mind, but you're not going to lose me Denley. I love you and I know one day we will be married but we have to keep busy for now so we don't go mad."

He pulled her into his arms and made her promise and then he held her like he didn't want to let her go.

He knew he couldn't change her mind and maybe it would be good for both of them so he sighed in resignation, "I'll make arrangements with Nick and we can travel with you as far as Sheffield.

Two days later and still no word from Mr. Fines they had Mr. Whitfield take them to Oxford instead of taking the coach. Nick was somewhat nervous about the possibility of having to face Mr. Sherman even though Denley had told him that he wouldn't need to do any talking. Ashley had seemed quiet and downcast since making her decision to get away so Denley began to worry about what she was thinking and wondering if there was more to her going to Sheffield than what she was saying. Was she thinking of moving there? Maybe she was going to be looking for a place to live. All these ideas were rolling around in his head, but he would move anywhere he had to just to be close to her as long as she didn't disappear and that was one thing Denley wasn't worried about. Mr. Whitfield made sure the luggage was stowed away on the train and headed back to Mrs. Thatcher's.

They boarded the train and found some seats. As the train started to jerk forward the whistle blew and Ashley thought it sounded rather sad this time. As they moved along the tracks they listened to the sounds of the train drowning out the idle chatter of other passengers. Ashley sat with her head resting on Denley's shoulder and he promised to make sure she made it to Josie's before re-boarding the train even if it meant staying one night in Sheffield. "I'm sure it won't be too much longer before Mr. Fines has some news for us. There will be a way around it. The visit with Josie will be good for you and will help you take your mind off the present situation. I should be back from Newcastle before you return so you can send a telegram and I'll pick you up from Oxford."

The train finally arrived and Denley helped Ashley off. They hired a carriage to take them to Josie's and Nick decided to give them some privacy so he waited at the station for Denley to return.

When the carriage arrived at the front of Josie's, Denley turned to Ashley and gave her a reassuring kiss and then helped her down and taking her by her hand he led her to the door. The carriage driver climbed down and unloaded her belongings. Denley had only met Josie on the one occasion and was able to meet her husband Charles this time. He seemed like a very pleasant man. After a quick greeting and being introduced to Charles, Denley had to return to the train station. One more kiss and a few comforting words and he left.

Denley booked Nick and himself into hotel rooms and told him to take his time settling in. When he was ready he could just knock on Denley's room and they would go for dinner. He would have to wait until the morning to go to the shipyard to collect the files on Nick and talk to a few of the men under his employment.

He wanted time to go over everything carefully before they went in to see Mr. Sherman

After his visit to the shipyard Denley stopped at his mothers. She was so surprised to see him but was hurt that he had stayed in a hotel. "I'm here on business and I'm not here with Ashley. I brought Nick Larson with me. I told you about him being injured in the shipyard. I need to go through more of father's old files and check out any paperwork on the shipyard that I may have missed before. I should just crate all the papers up and I can get them out of the house for you.

"Are you feeling better than you were in Harwell?"

"Not particularly. How is Ashley doing?"

"I'm worried about her. She's in Sheffield for a week and I don't know what's going on with her. She has been so withdrawn lately. She said she needed to get away and she left the children in Harwell. If I have to, I'll sell the shipyard and take her to America if that's what it takes to make her my wife."

"Denny darling you can't just leave again. I have barely had you back. I don't want you to move so far away, and what about Katie. She would grow up hardly knowing me."

"Mother you have to understand I will do whatever it takes. I refuse to lose Ashley and Katie, and now we have Hannah as well. We can talk later. I have to get back to the hotel so I can go over these papers with Nick. I want to get things settled and be back home before Ashley returns."

"You won't leave Newcastle without coming back to say good-bye will you."

"No, I can come by when I'm finished at Mr. Sherman's office."

Picking through the papers and pulling out any that looked like they would be helpful he gave his mother a hug and left. Back at the room he went through the papers from the shipyard and from his mothers and found the papers from the file giving the payout for each of the three families of the men killed and the payout for Nick Larson.

Denley talked to the police and had them waiting outside Mr. Sherman's office the next day. Denley asked Nick to wait five minutes before coming in. He wanted Mr. Sherman to think it was a friendly business meeting but the smile fell from his face when Denley told him he would like to introduce a business partner to him and he found himself standing face to face with Nick.

He cleared his throat and loosened his tie as if he was having trouble breathing. He started to back up a bit and stammered trying to come up with an explanation.

"There is nothing you can say to clear up what you have done. You were to pay Nick for injuries he received from the accident. I want you to figure out the amount and be sure to add the interest."

Like an obedient child he pulled out his books and started calculating the amount. He opened the safe in his office and counted out a large sum of notes and handed them to Denley, but Denley refused it. "You were to give it to Mr. Larson and that hasn't changed."

He handed the notes to Nick and mumbled an apology. Nick had never earned so much money in his entire life

"Did you make the payments to the families of the deceased or did you pocket that money as well?"

"They were paid in full."

"That was your last act in my employment. I have notified the legal authorities of all the money you have stolen from my father's company and they are waiting outside for you. I will take all the files pertaining to all my properties that you have managed and the ones of my mothers as well."

When all the business was finished Denley hired a carriage and had Nick taken back to the hotel and then he was taken to his mothers. When he arrived she refused to come out of her sleeping chamber and was told she had a headache. Insisting on seeing her in the capacity of a doctor he knocked and walked in. His mother was lying in bed and in quite a state. She was complaining of a headache and looking very distraught.

"Mother, what have you done to put yourself in such a state?"

"I just can't bear the idea of you moving to America, even that you would consider it. With William gone and now your father too it's just too much to bear. There are things you don't know, things I've never told anyone. In one way it will keep you here but I could lose you so easily and my heart is being pulled in two different directions. It feels as if it will rip in half." She was dabbing at the tears forming in her eyes.

"I don't know what you're talking about. What could be so bad that it would cause me to walk away from you? I'm sorry I left without a word before but I wouldn't do that again. I never imagined that you would take it the way you did." He was now sitting on the edge of her bed trying to reassure her and holding one of her hands.

"Hand me that small wooden box sitting on the bureau please." She motioned with her hand toward a small box only big enough to hold small trinkets. "Oh God forgive me, because you probably won't."

"Mother what have you done?" He was now getting worried as he handed her the box.

She fumbled with the small latch and lifted the lid. There were a few pieces of paper in it and she pulled them out. She held them to her chest and looked at him and then with a slight hesitation she handed them to him to read. "Please don't hate me; I couldn't bear it if you did." She began to cry as he took the papers from her.

Slowly he read the one paper. Then he read it again. Color drain from his face as he looked at her in disbelief. "I don't understand how you could sit facing me before Fathers death and tell me that I was the child of both of you and then hand me a paper that tells me I'm not related to either of you. I can see why I don't need to move to America though it's sounding really good at this moment," then raising his voice, "what I need is an explanation. I can't think of anything you could possibly say to make things between us better. But go on, amuse me. Give me a reason why I should stay."

The paper he was holding revealed his real mothers name is Tessa Hampton.

Pauline cleared her throat and trying to remain calm she tried to explain without leaving anything out. "What I told you about your father getting drunk and me taking William and going to my mother's was true. She didn't know I was coming and I didn't know she had a visitor. Her friend's daughter had gotten herself in trouble and she was sent to mothers to have her baby. They were trying to keep it very quiet to save their families reputation. Her name is Tessa Hampton. She was to have her baby and give it up for adoption and then go back home. My mother handed you to me the instant you were born to tend to you. I wrapped you in a blanket and fell in love with you. You were so tiny." Her eyes sparkled as she was remembering that moment. "I decided to keep you. Given the size you were and the time I was away it worked that I could pass you off as Willard's if I needed to. To have had an affair with another man I would have had to have done it within days of my arriving at mothers. So I didn't lie to him about an affair; just the part about passing you off as ours. He refused to give me another child and I wanted one so desperately.

It seemed like a wonderful idea. He accused me of having an affair the second I walked in the door when I returned with William. He refused to consider even the possibility that you could be his from that one night or that you might have been orphaned or given up for adoption He just accused me. So I fabricated a story and all I had to do was stick to what I told him. That was easy because I was so hurt and mad at him for what he had done to me and for the hurtful words he said to me when I had returned. I never legally adopted you because I was afraid your father would see the papers, so all I have is the papers that Tessa and the Doctor did up for me. If it ever became a problem I would be able to do it at a later date. And that is the whole story." The other paper he was holding was in an envelope with her name on the front. He recognized it to be the one from the day the will was read.

"More is explained in the other one you are holding."

Denley stood and stared at her for a moment holding the paper and the envelope and then he turned and walked out without a word to her.

She called after him but he continued walking. His thoughts were of confusion and anger all mixed up and he realized that Ashley may not even want to marry him when she finds out he is not only illegitimate but he doesn't even carry his father's name. The only name on that paper is Tessa Hampton.

Back at the hotel he told Nick he was not feeling well and just wanted to rest and he hoped he didn't mind getting dinner on his own. He sat on the bed and undid his tie. It had been a long day and it really wasn't that late. He wasn't sure he wanted to read the other letter but he also knew he had to before he showed it to Ashley.

They took the first train in the morning and Denley wanted to get off in Sheffield and see how Ashley was doing. "I might stay a night or two."

"Well, I'm gonna keep goin if ya don't mind. I'm wantin to share this new fortune with my Rosie."

By the time he was knocking on Charles and Josie's door Denley couldn't believe how his stomach was tied up in knots. The possible idea of being rejected by Ashley now was playing on his mind and making him sick.

Josie answered the door and was surprised to see Denley. "Is Ashley in, I mean is she feeling well?"

"Yes. Where are my manners, come in. I'm just so surprised to see you. Ashley said you would be home before her but we never expected you to stop on your way back. Are you in a hurry to catch the train again?"

"No, I told Nick I might stay a day or two here in Sheffield."

"Charles is in the den. I'll put some tea on. Ashley is lying down for a bit and if you don't mind I would like her to rest." She led Denley into the den to visit while she went to do up a tray.

The men talked about there professions for some time but Denley could tell there was something on Charles mind. Finally Charles could help it no longer, "You can tell me it's none of my business but, well Ashley has been quite reserved this visit and very tired and I'm just hoping you didn't stop with bad news."

"I do have news but it will depend on how Ashley feels about it and I would rather talk to her about it first. I am hopeful that she will take it as good news."

"I understand. Shall we join Josie in the sitting room?"

Ashley came down after she had freshened up and was surprised when Denley stood as she entered the room. To his delight she rushed into his arms and seemed to be back to herself at least from what he could make of her greeting. "How long have you been here? You should have had Josie wake me."

"I wanted to but Josie wouldn't hear of it. She said you needed your rest and that's okay. I might stay a few days here in Sheffield. I would like to have a private talk with you though."

Charles offered the use of the den to them. "You know where to find it. Just make yourself comfortable."

They went in and leaving the door open they sat next to each other. "I have to show you something and depending on your reaction will decide whether we get married or not."

By his words and the look on his face she was expecting the worst.

Denley handed her the paper, "This is our consent to be married if you will still have me once you read what it says."

She read the paper over and then handed it back to him. "Denley your still the man I fell in love with and this doesn't change who you are. This is just a name on a paper. What's in the envelope?"

"This was given to mother the day father's will was read. He opened the envelope and began to read out loud, "My dearest Pauline: I have much in my life to be sorry for. The word sorry was not in my vocabulary when alive so perhaps it will be easier to put on paper. I realize I made your life miserable. I had to do some reflecting back and what I saw of myself was not something I am proud of. Some of the things you wanted I crushed shortly after we were married and that was wrong of me. I accused you of being unfaithful even though you begged me to believe it wasn't true. Whether that was true or not I should have tried to make your life more endurable but instead I treated you and Denley terribly. In my favoring William you were forced to treat Denley differently. I know you held some sort of secret from me and I wish I could have been the kind of person you could have told.

I don't know how long you will keep your secret from him but I hope if ever you have to tell him; he will be understanding and more forgiving than me. If it is found out that he is not a Radcliff I want it to be known that the inheritance left to him is still to him as our son.

Love Willard

If only Father was the type of person Mother could have been open with. If she could have told him the secret she held for so many years things would have been so different. Maybe he wouldn't have hated me so much if he had known the truth."

"The last thing he requested is that if you found out the truth you would be forgiving. Where's mother Pauline now?"

"I left her lying in her room. I just couldn't face her after what I found out. It wasn't only the lie, but it makes me wonder what are Tessa Hampton and my real father like."

"This had to almost destroy her to give this to you. She's carried this secret for so many years; she could have just kept it to herself but as it is we can get married. Denley you have to make things right with her. She's the one who loved you and raised you. We have to get past this because whether you want a relationship with her or not she is still Katie's grandmother and she has a right to be part of Katie's life. It will be easier if you are at least on speaking terms."

Deep down he knew Ashley was right and the fact that his father wanted him to be forgiving made it difficult to be any other way. He gave Ashley a kiss on the cheek, "I think I know that but it's just such a shock to find out I'm not who I...Well I'm just trying to come to terms with it. I wasn't even sure you would want me after finding out I'm a bastard. This all seems so unreal."

"Don't say it like that. It sounds so harsh and you will never hear me call you that. I am sure Mother Pauline will feel better now that that is no longer hanging over her." Then with an excited squeal that took him totally by surprise and had Charles and Josie running into the room she exclaimed, "We can get married! We have to go tomorrow. We have a wedding to plan again." By the time they left the den Maddie and Caroline were awake and had come downstairs. Denley was prepared to get a room at a hotel but Charles told him they would be able to find a room for him.

Finally back at Elizabeth's they rushed in to tell them the news. Ashley was her cheerful self again and greeted the children with hugs and for the first time she handed Katie to Denley and told her to give him a kiss because he was going to be her father.

That night up in her room she stood looking at her wedding dress hanging up and was thrilled to think that she would actually be wearing it in a week's time. She needed to send a couple of telegrams first thing in the morning. She wasn't sure how Denley would feel about it, but she was going to invite Mother Pauline to the wedding. It would be easy to explain away as she is Katie's grandmother and Katie would want her to come. She was also sure that Denley would want her there even if he didn't want to admit it. There was no way she was going to allow them to go too long before making peace.

The garden was being readied again and the baking was getting done leaving the smell of freshly baked pies and pastries of all sorts filling the air, and you couldn't help but hang around close to the kitchen just for the pleasant aroma that wafted by. Elizabeth was fussing over every little detail and spared no expense on making everything perfect as she would have done for a daughter, had she been blessed with one of her own. Maggie was busy with tending to the children and helping out with other preparations. Ellen was taking care of the final touches inside.

13
The Big Day

Saturday started with a light shower in the morning but promised to clear in time for the wedding. Elizabeth was panicking because they had to wait for the showers to stop before they could have the benches set out and she was a bundle of nerves. Ashley had to finally tell her everything was perfect and to calm down.

It was easier to say than do as Ashley too was a bundle of nerves. She never in her life expected to have to do this twice.

Maggie had promised to bathe the children and have them dressed and ready on time. Before beginning to get herself ready she had Maggie come to her room. "I bought you a gift, a thank-you for all your help. I hope it fits." She handed her a package and Maggie was thrilled to open it to a new fancy dress.

"I've never had such a beautiful dress before." It was an emerald green with sparkling glass buttons, short puff sleeves, and a few soft pleats at the waist of the skirt allowing it to flow in nice straight lines.

"Maggie before you go can I ask you to help me lace up my corset?"

"Yes, I would be happy to help you with that."

Ashley went and quickly put it on and turned her back to Maggie so she could begin. Then with a knock on the door

Elizabeth slipped in and excused Maggie and she finished lacing her up like a mother would do for a daughter. This too was something new for Elizabeth. She then helped her into her dress and did up all the buttons down the back and remarked several times that there were sure a lot of them. After Elizabeth left the room Ashley finished with her silk stockings. She did her hair up using the hair pins that had been her mothers to hold it in place but left some soft curls loose around her face. With the finishing touches done she listened to the commotion going on as invited guests were being welcomed and escorted through to the garden. She heard Denley's voice and was relieved to know he had arrived. Then she heard Mother Pauline's voice and was thrilled that she came. She slipped into a seat at the back just before the ceremony was to start. Hopefully Denley won't mind but she had that covered too. This day was important to Katie and she would want her grandmother here to share it. Denley noticed his mother slip in and asked John Kerrington to have her seated in the front because he knew that is where she belonged.

There was a light tap on the door, "are you almost ready?"

Ashley opened the door quickly. "Josie you came! I can't believe it; you're actually here."

"Of coarse I'm here. You can thank Charles. He knew how badly I wanted to be here so he made the arrangements with his mother to stay for a few days and help to look after things. Now…are you ready?"

"As ready as I'll ever be."

"Give me a minute to get down to my seat and then you can come"

"Josie wait. You can walk with me. I don't have anyone to give me away and I'm not asking you to do that, but, you can walk with me down to Denley. Please say you'll do it; I'm so nervous."

"Ok. Ok. I'll walk with you just stay calm. Denley seems like a very caring and gentle man." She arranged Ashley's dress behind her and opened the door. They walked down the stairs with Ashley train and veil floating gracefully behind and Denley was standing just inside the doors to watch her come down. Then Josie walked ahead of them and He took Ashley gently by the arm and led her out to the garden. When they made their way to the front Denley took Ashley by the hand and took a deep nervous breath.

Ashley looked at Denley and smiled. He looked so handsome and he had the biggest smile on his face too. He was wearing a black pin stripe suite and had a small flower tucked in the lapel of his coat.

After all the "I dos, and you may now kiss the bride," his mother went up to wish them well and Denley quickly but hesitantly he gave her a hug and then he gave her a second hug and whispered something in her ear. He then turned to Ashley, "You are a crafty woman but I'm so glad you invited her to come. They visited with the rest of their guests and opened their gifts.

Elizabeth offered to have all the gifts taken to their house if they left the key with her. "I left your gift up in your room."

Up in her bedroom was an envelope on the bed with Ashley and Denley's name on it. They sat on the bed and Ashley opened it and pulled out a card. On it was written:

Ashley you have brought so much life into this house since you were brought here. Having Katie here has also been such a blessing. You can't even imagine how much all of us will miss you.

Denley we have enjoyed watching you care for Ashley and have watched you fall in love with her. I think we knew you loved her before she herself knew, and the way Katie has taken to you is heart warming. I am so happy that you chose to live nearby so we can see you often. My gift to you is the bedroom furniture. I won't have it any other way. Katie was born in this room and it is only natural that you accept it. Be happy.

Love Elizabeth.

Denley put his arms around Ashley and pulled her close. "Well Mrs. Denley Hampton Radcliff…do you realize we're sitting on our bed with the door closed?" He kissed her softly on the neck.

"Yes Mr. Denley Hampton Radcliff I am quite aware of that, and do you know we have guests' downstairs waiting for us to return. We also have a coach that leaves in just over an hour."

He groaned in resignation and standing up he pulled her to her feet. "Speaking of guests and coaches, I know Josie coming was a big surprise so why don't I let you visit longer with her and we can sneak off and catch a later coach or one tomorrow? It is unlikely she will be able to come this way too often."

"I knew there was a reason I married you. You're so thoughtful."

"Speaking of thoughtful; what did you whisper in your mother's ear?"

"That I love her and that will never change and how happy I was that she came."

They headed downstairs and found Josie amusing Elizabeth with tales of when Ashley and she were in school together. They made a point of visiting with everyone and thanking them for the gifts they received.

When John Kerrington seen Hannah he thought he recognized her as a child he had treated for an ear infection. Denley explained how they came to have her and asked him if her mother might have said anything about her father or given a name but this too seemed like a dead end. "I do remember her mother seemed to have a lot of bruises on her face and arms though." But that was all he could tell Denley.

They enjoyed their afternoon and watched as Maggie spent most of her time chasing after Katie and Hannah. Mother Pauline doted on both girls because they were rarely separated. Nick and Rosie couldn't stay long as they had lodgers and needed to get back and let them in. John stayed a little longer but he had a house call that had to be made. It was actually one of Denley's patients but he was taking over until Denley returned from his honeymoon. It was planned that Josie would stay at Elizabeth's for the night as Denley's place had been rearranged to hold the four of them until they moved into their house after they returned from their honeymoon. By 6:00 pm they were giving Katie and Hannah hugs and kisses and saying goodbye.

They had decided to leave in the morning when they would be well rested (hopefully), so they headed to Denley's place for the night. He carried her over the threshold and into the cramped small entrance. He gave Ashley a gentle kiss on her cheek and then moved towards her waiting lips. They moved away from the door and into the bedroom. He began unbuttoning Ashley's dress and slowly stripping off the layers. Then he lifted her up and carried her to the bed. He disappeared for a couple of minutes and Ashley quickly slipped into a thin silk gown embellished with fancy lace and satin ribbons. Denley brought in a tray with a bowl of sweets and two glasses of champagne, his coat and tie were already removed and he placed the tray down and sat on the edge of the bed and unbuttoned his shirt. He pulled his shoes and socks of and slipped out of his suite pants.

Trying not to be embarrassed as he made himself comfortable next to her she finally broke the silence. "It has occurred to me that you have already seen every inch of my body."

"Yes but I was busy trying to save your life so really it doesn't count because I wasn't looking at you like that. I can't believe I finally have you all to myself." As the evening wore on she cuddled into his arms and they ate the sweets and drank their champagne.

They left for the coach early the next morning and headed for the train station. It was going to be a long day but much more enjoyable than when they had Katie with them the first time they traveled to Newcastle. Nothing mattered to them except they were finally together, after all the turmoil they were legally married.

The first few days they enjoyed some of the upper class dinners, strolled through beautifully pruned gardens, went to the theater and enjoyed an opera performance. Each morning they would head down to the restaurant for breakfast. Ashley had her heart set on finding the perfect piano. Denley had never heard her play but when she was looking at them she plunked on the keys and tried playing a tune or two that she remembered. She played when she was in school and wanted to teach Katie, and if Hannah remained with them for any length of time she would teach her as well. When she finally decided on the one she wanted Denley made all the arrangements for having it shipped by train to coincide with when he knew they would be back in Harwell. They enjoyed strolling along the streets and looking in the small shops.

Before they left Newcastle they went to the barn. Denley wanted to see how Karl was doing with Katie's horse. She was not quite as spirited as last time. He was just starting to get her used to having a saddle on her back. "I think I'm going to buy us riding horses and we are going to learn how to ride. Do you think you would like that?

"I've been on a horse before. Not too much but it was ok. It's really not the kind of thing I like but you should do it if you want. Maybe with you I would enjoy it more, if not at least your would be able to take Katie and Hannah riding; when they're older of coarse.

In Sheffield Ashley picked out a leather chair for the library but to get it in the cognac color she wanted they would have to wait on it. It would be delivered when it was ready. "I hope you are finished buying furniture," he teased "we bought a house fully furnished."

Josie insisted on them staying with their family for the night, and wouldn't take "no" for an answer. Charles was a stone Mason and had been responsible for the designing and building of some very large homes and bridges so he was working when they first arrived but they had a nice visit in the evening.

Josie wasn't feeling well in the morning and Denley and Ashley were getting ready to leave but Denley was concerned that she was looking a little pale. Charles chalked it up to all the excitement of being at their wedding and now having them stay for a visit even though it was a short one. Denley wasn't too sure about it and insisted she see her doctor as soon as possible.

Charles laughed, "I guess you never quit being a doctor do you?"

Just as he was about to answer, Josie stood up and then she doubled over in agonizing pain and fell back onto the sofa she had been sitting on. Charles was immediately by her side and Denley was sending Ashley to get his medical bag.

"Maddie be a doll and take Caroline up stairs to the nursery." Charles was trying to stay calm and he didn't want the children to see their mother in pain.

Denley was asking where the pain was the worst and had her lie down so he could feel her abdomen. He asked if she had felt this pain before and started asking a few personal questions. "Could you possibly be pregnant?"

"I never gave it a thought. I was so excited about attending your wedding and spending the time with Ashley; I'm never regular so it's possible, and now that you mention it, I very well could be."

Denley gave Charles a look to see how he was taking the news. "Well it is bed rest for you for a while and you should have your doctor call and check on you. If there is any bleeding you should send for him immediately."

Ashley wanted to stay in Sheffield an extra day to make sure Josie would be alright. She spent the day making sure Josie followed the doctor's orders and told her about the first time she met Denley and he told her she had to stay in bed. "If you think that's bad, I was in a strangers home and feeling very embarrassed about it. It all turned out good though. Look what I got out of it, a dear friend that is like a mother to me in many ways and something totally unexpected. I found love, and I didn't ever think I would feel that again.

The next morning with one more warning of staying in bed and getting rested they said their goodbyes and left for the train. "I'll send you a letter in a few days, once we're settled into our new home.

They could see the clouds rolling in and they knew there was a storm brewing. "Hopefully it won't reach as far as Oxford." Denley was concerned because they had to switch to the coach and there was no way the coach would run if the conditions worsened.

Ashley leaned up against his shoulder and looked out the train window watching as the storm seemed to intensify the closer they got to Oxford. When they stepped off the train the storm hit them even though they were slightly sheltered between the station house and the train. They realized the storm was worse than it looked and there would be no chance of the coaches running until morning. They rushed into the station house to get out of the storm and Denley checked at the ticket booth to see what time the earliest coach would leave in the morning. They were now anxious to get home especially considering the storm seemed to intensify more in that direction. All they could do is wait it out. From the safety of the station they watched out the window as the lightning flashed across the sky and the sound of the thunder rumbled behind. If not for the fact that the summer had been fairly dry for the most part and they were desperately wanting to be home it would have been a spectacular show. The wind was blowing and the rain was pouring down so they waited until the rain slowed to make a run for a hotel. It was hard to get any sleep because of the noise from the storm. They were also restless and anxious for the safety of everyone at Elizabeth's.

They were relieved when morning finally came and the storm had passed. The coaches would be running and they rushed to get ready.

They watched out the windows of the coach in disbelief at the amount of trees down and the damage to property. This added to their desire to be home as quickly as the horse's legs would move but the roads were muddy and there were branches over in some places that needed to be cleared, slowing the pace. When they finally reached Harwell Denley rushed to the stable to have his horse and carriage readied while Ashley waited as their trunk and carpet bags were being unloaded. It felt like an eternity before they were finally making their way through the big fancy gates at Elizabeth's. Some of the trees that lined the driveway were down but the branches had already been cleared enough to get through. Their first glimpse of the house was enough to send shivers up their spine in shear panic. A big tree had fallen against the house and had taken out a number of rooms on the upper floor. Ashley gripped Denley's hand, "It's the children's room."

Denley snapped the reigns to move the horses quicker and when he pulled them to a stop they were out and running for the house afraid of what they might see.

Running in they were calling the children's names and before they could get any other names out Maggie appeared and the children ran out from behind her into their arms. Ashley buried her face in Katie's hair thankful for their safety and Denley lifted Hannah up and encircled the three of them with a protective and thankful embrace. They made their way farther into the house to the kitchen where everyone was gathered. Elizabeth had a few scratches on her arms and was still shaken from the idea that the children could have been killed had it not been for Maggie. The children weren't in their room when the tree came crashing down in it. They had been unsettled with the storm and Maggie had brought them downstairs to sleep with her on one of the big comfortable chairs.

Ellen was hurt the most with some cuts needing stitches and some bruising to her face. A branch from a different tree made its way through her window and landed on her as she was trying to get ready for bed.

The cottage in the back that the Whitfield's live in sustained minimal damage and would take very little effort to repair but Elizabeth's home would need extensive repairs and she was not able to think that far ahead.

Denley went out to get his medical bag from the carriage and spotted John coming down the drive. He waited for John to catch up and they walked in together.

"I was just coming to check on everyone here to see how they faired. When did you get back?"

"We had to spend the night in Oxford. We were on the first carriage out this morning. We have just been back long enough to hear the details. Thankfully there are no serious injuries. Come on in. Ellen took the worst of it and needs a few stitches but it could have been a lot worse. Maggie had brought the children down stairs and it's a good thing because that's their room," he pointed to where the most damage had occurred.

"Elizabeth is going to have to move out until the house can be repaired. Has she given any thought to what she will do?" John was sizing up the damage as they walked in.

"Not yet, and I don't think she is even ready to talk about it. We will have to make arrangements fairly quickly though. There is no way she can stay here."

John tended to Elizabeth's scratches, cleaning them out and wrapping them. She started to complain about some pain in her left arm. It wasn't broke but she must have strained some of the muscles when she was pulling the branch off of Ellen. While he was doing that Denley was cleaning out Ellen's cuts and getting ready to put some stitches in the deeper ones. She was feeling rather faint at the whole idea. Maggie took the children to a different room thankful that she didn't have to stay and watch.

14
Getting Settled

Elizabeth was in no shape to make decisions so Denley took over. He had Maggie and Ashley gather up some of the things Elizabeth would need and John helped clear the branches and glass out of the way for Ellen to collect some of her clothes. Denley tried to get to some of Katie and Hannah's things but he only grabbed things close to the door. He didn't feel it was safe to go in too far before some supports were put in place. Once everything was gathered up and loaded into the carriage Denley helped Ashley into it and handed her Snowball and then he climbed up beside her. They would all move into the house on Willow Brook Road and Mr. Whitfield would follow with the other carriage and bring along Elizabeth, Maggie, Ellen and the children.

Denley quickly carried Ashley over the thresh hold before everyone else arrived

Elizabeth and Ellen were given strict orders to do no lifting so the majority of the unpacking was left to Maggie and Ashley

Denley was in need of John's help and was hoping to bring a few of the beds over from Elizabeth's as they didn't have enough with having so many extra people for a while. He was beginning to watch the house slowly be transformed into a home and was thankful that they bought this house.

Ashley thought it strange that someone would knock on the door while they were busy moving in. There had been workers coming and going but they had all finished their work and had been paid. She opened the door to a young man who introduced himself as Earl Shaw. She guessed him to be about 5'10, and possibly somewhere between 19 to 21 years of age. He had a crop of thick blond hair and a ruddy complexion. His clothes were clean but nothing fancy. His shirt was a blue plaid and he was wearing coveralls with a patch on one knee. He had a solid build but he was not over weight.

"If Mr. Radcliff is in, I was wondering if I might have a word with him."

She opened the door to allow him to enter and closing the door behind him she asked if he would wait while she found Denley.

Earl Shaw extended his hand and introduced himself. "I've been working on the clean up for you but I was wondering if by chance you've hired your stable hand yet. I'm good with horses and I know my way around all their tack and gear. I'm looking for a stable job and hoping that it will come with some type of living quarters and meals. I'm sorry I don't come with much of a recommendation. I have only worked in the stables with my father but I've been doing it since I was old enough to handle a pitch fork. All I can say is you wouldn't be disappointed, I'm dependable and I work hard."

"I haven't hired anyone yet and I'll give you a try for a month and see how it goes. There is a room attached to the barn and it has a bed and a small cupboard to put clothes and belongings in. I'm really not in the need of a stable hand quite yet but if you want to move in and start cleaning up the area I'll start you off at 7 shillings a week and when I increase my number of horses I'll take it up to 9 shillings. I could use your help moving some of our belongings and there will be plenty of work to do if you're any good with a hammer."

"Thank-you sir, thank-you very much. You won't be disappointed."

"Put your things away and I'll put you to work right now. We are in the process of moving in and because of the storm we have more to do than planned.

Between John, Earl and Denley they managed to get enough beds set up and were able to move the matching pieces of bedroom furniture that Elizabeth had given as a wedding gift.

Ashley felt a sense of satisfaction though they still had to hire at least two more people. They needed a cook and someone to do the cleaning. Denley hadn't said if he wanted a butler but it was unlikely at this point. He had been raised with a butler in the house when he was growing up but had been away from if for some time and really didn't want that type of life for himself or his family. If she could find the two for in the house she would have time to tend to the children. She would wait until Elizabeth was feeling up to going with her to the orphanage to see if they had any girls ready to be given work. Denley had told her that it would be her responsibility to hire her cook and maids as it would be her that would have to deal with them the most.

Maggie made up Ellen's bed first. She needed to lie down and get some rest and Elizabeth's room was next. They had all gotten very little sleep because of the storm and with all the work they had to get done everyone was retiring early.

Maggie settled the girls into their new room and sat with them until they settled in.

The next day the rest of Denley's belongings were moved to their house and his place was cleaned. Dr. Kerrington decided to take it over; he had stayed with his sister long enough. It was good to have a doctor living directly above the clinic that could be available all hours of the day or night in case of emergencies.

When Elizabeth was feeling up to going to Oxford the following day Earl was more than eager to be given his first chance to take them on an outing and he did quite well. He knew his way around Oxford and his manners were impeccable. Elizabeth was quite impressed.

When they arrived at the orphanage they had to wait until the head mistress was available. They were led into a room and sat down. While they were waiting they noticed the small children being taken outside for some fresh air and exercise. When the head mistress entered she introduced herself. "My name is Beverly Stone. What can I do for you ladies today?"

They explained their reason for being there and Elizabeth told her that she had gotten Maggie through them.

"I remember. Maggie had been with us for quite a few years and we all missed her when she left. And how is she working out for you?"

"I have been extremely happy with her. We are hoping you have a couple of girls with the same 'ready to please' attitude that she has."

"I have three young girls ready. What exactly will be required of them?"

Ashley now spoke up. "I will need one that's good in the kitchen as a cook, and one that will be good with children and cleaning.

"Janet is very good in the kitchen. Her mother was quite ill and she had to do all the cooking at a young age. When her mother died she was brought here and has worked in the kitchen with our cooks. The other two have no cooking sense in them but if you want someone good with children I would recommend Beatrice over Helen but you may talk to them both. I will have all three girls brought in."

Janet is brought in first. She is almost seventeen. She has dark brown hair, sparkly bright brown eyes, and a straight nose. She has dimples when she smiles and that reveals white teeth a little crooked but not unsightly. She looks older than she is which indicates a maturity about her that is intriguing.

"How do you feel about cooking meals for two children and at least eight adults at the start but will eventually be about six adults? I would need to know that you can handle it. I can supply help from other staff in the cleaning up as long as you can cook with confidence. We can go over menus at the start and you would be able to talk to Elizabeth's cook if you need ideas until you're settled."

Janet replied with confidence, "I believe I can handle the cooking. Who will be responsible for keeping the kitchen stocked?"

"You would be; however there may be times when you can send someone else with a list if you can't get away. We are very close to town so you shouldn't have a problem with that. You will also need to get along with other staff."

She gave a slight curtsey and was excused from the room.

Beatrice was next to be interviewed and she was a bubbly energetic girl of just sixteen. She had sandy blond hair that she wore in a french braid at the back. She had green eyes, a turned up nose and a cheery smile.

"I need someone who can do regular work, laundry, beds, dusting...You need to be good with children and when needed, help in the kitchen with dishes. This means you will need to accept assignments from the cook from time to time. Do you have any questions?"

"No Mrs. Radcliff. I love children and I know I can handle the tasks. I would be happy to be given the opportunity to prove it."

After meeting Helen and going over the same things as she did with Beatrice she was dismissed and the head mistress gave Ashley and Elizabeth a moment to talk things over. Ashley thought Janet and Beatrice would be the obvious two to hire and then asked Elizabeth's opinion. "That is what I was thinking too."

After making her final decision she asked the head mistress if she felt the girls could be ready to go within half an hour. "That won't be a problem. If you'll excuse me I'll go tell the girls to say their good-byes and they can be ready in about 15 minutes."

With both girls smiling they gave the head mistress a goodbye hug and she presented each one with a book as a keepsake. Ashley asked that they wait outside and when the door was closed she made a considerable donation to the orphanage.

When she joined the girls and Elizabeth outside Ashley introduced them to Earl and he stowed their belongings away. "We need to find a shop where I can buy the girls each a uniform and I will get you a pair of new coveralls and a work shirt."

They found a dress in a medium shade of grey for Janet and for Beatrice a green dress in a soft shade, both made of cotton and Ashley found white aprons and bonnets for them. By the time they had bought the dresses and found the coveralls and shirt for Earl it was time to head back to Harwell.

The girls were anxious to see their new surroundings and have a tour of the house on Willow Brook Road.

Earl took care to see that the horse was un-harnessed, groomed and fed. He was happy for the opportunity to prove himself. It would be nice to have someone to talk to at meal times. He always had his father to eat his meals with, but nothing was the same since his mother's death and it was time for him to get out on his own. It was his father that had suggested talking to Dr. Denley.

Walking into the house Katie and Hannah rushed to greet Ashley and Elizabeth and stopped short when they realized they hadn't walked in alone. Quickly making shy Hannah rushed back and hid behind Maggie's skirt but Katie was a little braver and peeked around Ashley but staying close.

Beatrice knelt down to her level, "I am guessing your name is Katie. Your mother has told me all about you," then looking in the direction of Hannah who was now bravely taking a peek from a safe distance, "and you must be Hannah the little shy girl I have heard about. Won't you come and say hello?" She extended her arms as if to offer a hug. When both girls refused to accept she stood up and smiled at them. "That's okay, once you get to know me you'll find I'm a friendly person.

Janet said hello to both girls but you could tell she was less interested in gaining their affections.

"Maggie, will you please show these young ladies through the house and where their rooms are. You probably know each other and you may have a little catching up to do so I'll leave you to it. After they are settled they can join me in the study for some instructions."

Maggie led them up the stairs and Elizabeth and Ashley headed to the kitchen.

Twenty minutes later the girls joined her in the study and Ashley indicated for them to take a seat opposite her. "Janet, I'll begin with you. You will be expected to plan and prepare the meals and to keep the kitchen clean and orderly. If you need help with the cleaning and Beatrice is not otherwise engaged you can have her give you a hand. Mrs. Thatcher's cook is just a short walk away and I am sure she will be more than willing to help you for the first few days. I believe she may be in the kitchen now. She has kindly offered to be here for tomorrow's breakfast but after that she will only be helping with the lunch and supper until her work returns to normal so I suggest you go ask her what time you will be expected to start tomorrow.

Beatrice I thank you for your attempt at talking with the girls. You will find by tomorrow they will be less shy. As I explained to both of you on our ride back, Maggie and Ellen will be working here with you until they can return to Mrs. Thatcher's. You're work will begin when Maggie's does so I suggest you ask her what time she gets up as that will also be your time.

Janet I will start you off at three shillings a week. Beatrice you will start off at two and a half shillings and we will see how you are working out. I do have some basic ground rules that will apply to you both. I do not expect men in your sleeping chambers and if you choose to marry you will be expected to keep your courtship proper. Get pregnant and you're gone if unmarried. Drinking during your working hours is prohibited unless we are celebrating and you are invited to join us. If you drink you are expected to be able to work the next day. Do either of you have any questions?"

Both girls were smiling with the wages offered, "We have no questions at this time Mrs. Radcliff but if we think of anything we will be sure to ask."

The girls were dismissed and Beatrice went to find Maggie. She was especially interested in gaining the children's trust. Janet headed to the kitchen to find out what time she needed to start in the morning and then went in search of Maggie as well.

Denley had taken the opportunity to meet both of the young ladies and thought Beatrice would do well with the children. He too was concerned about whether it might be a bit much to expect Janet to handle all the cooking but she wasn't concerned at all.

In the evening Beatrice and Maggie took the children up to get them ready and tucked into bed while Janet headed to the kitchen to start working on a menu and list of things she would need.

Ellen was going to leave in the morning to visit her family until Elizabeth's home was repaired and by then she would be able to return to work. Both Elizabeth and Ellen had retired to their rooms to give Denley and Ashley some privacy. It had been a big change and would take some time before Elizabeth's home would be repaired. They had hired a crew to do the work and Mr. Whitfield was overseeing it.

Denley put a small fire on and poured two glasses of wine. They sat quietly snuggled together unwinding and enjoying the satisfaction of what they had accomplished over the last couple of days. Ashley felt good because in some small way she was able to help Elizabeth in her time of distress as she had helped Ashley so long ago. They hadn't intended on moving in so quickly and there was still much to be done but they were home.